SUNDAY DRIVE TO GUN CLUB ROAD

SUNDAY DRIVE *to* GUN CLUB ROAD

Stories
MARION QUEDNAU

NIGHTWOOD EDITIONS

2021

Copyright © Marion Quednau, 2021

ALL RIGHTS RESERVED. No part of this publication may be reproduced, stored in a retrieval system or transmitted, in any form or by any means, without prior permission of the publisher or, in the case of photocopying or other reprographic copying, a licence from Access Copyright, the Canadian Copyright Licensing Agency, www.accesscopyright.ca, info@accesscopyright.ca.

Nightwood Editions
P.O. Box 1779
Gibsons, BC VON 1V0
Canada
www.nightwoodeditions.com

COVER DESIGN: Topshelf Creative
COVER PHOTO: Jp Valery on Unsplash
TYPOGRAPHY: Carleton Wilson

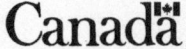 Canada Council   Conseil des Arts
for the Arts   du Canada

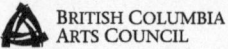 

Nightwood Editions acknowledges the support of the Canada Council for the Arts, the Government of Canada, and the Province of British Columbia through the BC Arts Council.

This book has been produced on 100% post-consumer recycled, ancient-forest-free paper, processed chlorine-free and printed with vegetable-based dyes.

Printed and bound in Canada.

LIBRARY AND ARCHIVES CANADA CATALOGUING IN PUBLICATION

Title: Sunday drive to Gun Club Road / Marion Quednau.
Names: Quednau, Marion, author.
Description: Short stories.
Identifiers: Canadiana (print) 20200352016 | Canadiana (ebook) 20200352067 |
    ISBN 9780889713987 (softcover) | ISBN 9780889713994 (HTML)
Classification: LCC PS8583.U337 S86 2021 | DDC C813/.54—dc23

A story, a story!
(Let it go. Let it come.)
—Anne Sexton

What matters we only tell ourselves.
—Charles Wright

CONTENTS

Snow Man 9

Garage Sale 23

Sunday Drive to Gun Club Road 33

Ex-Racehorses 49

Like a Bride 61

Onion 77

Twine 93

Men Shout 119

Two Birds, One Stone 131

For What It's Worth 145

Found to Be Missing 159

The Reading 187

Small Glory 195

Acknowledgements 205

About the Author 207

SNOW MAN

"I've seen some wacky things, but this beats them all," Harold said. He was looking out their front window at the man across the street. The new neighbour.

The man had a few years on them—that's what Kate thought. She was better at guessing these things: the size of a shirt just by looking at it, or the number of carrots needed in a stew for twenty family browsers. So if she guessed fifties, late, Harold would tend to believe her.

He supposed she thought so because of a receding hairline, largish brow, slightly stooped shoulders—but of course the fellow was looking down. He was looking at the fresh covering of snow in his front yard, several inches of the white stuff, smooth as a linen tablecloth. But apparently not smooth enough. For the man was prodding at the snow, reaching and pulling back gingerly, with a rake. He was raking the snow.

"What do you think? The absent-minded professor type?" Harold asked. Despite the sub-zero weather, their new neighbour was wearing only a thin trench coat, the sort worn to a business luncheon.

He didn't have a clue what this fellow was up to, but Kate did. "He's looking for something," she said. To Kate it was obvious.

The house had stood empty for months. It was one of those fake-Tudor suburban fantasies dreamed up by some developer in the seventies, stucco and fake beams, and all the wrong shape. Harold thought it probably leaked. He had said so several times over the months the For Sale sign had beckoned potential buyers.

"I know what he's lost," Harold muttered as he reluctantly turned away. "His marbles, that's what." He couldn't stand there all day watching a cracked neighbour.

"Maybe it's a family heirloom, his grandfather's fob, that sort of thing," Kate said. She watched as the man thoroughly crisscrossed the yard in a rigorous pattern. She said she could feel the man's regret.

"Yeah, he's misplaced his family jewels," Harold said, sputtering at his own bad taste. "Right."

* * * * *

They were having a Christmas party. The incoming snow had slowed to a nice drifting flake or two, just enough to make people arrive early and not drink too much before venturing home. That's what Kate hoped.

Friends they'd known for as long as they'd lived in the small town adjoining the city had all shown up. Their children were mostly teens and off doing their own thing, but a few late starters had brought a child or two with them. Sitters were hard to find at this time of year.

Food was abundant, wine and hot toddies in hand, conversations bright and sassy with annual teasing. "Yeah, well with the girth of a horse, all you need is sleigh bells, my King of

Shortbread." "It takes one good nag to know one," was thrown back. But it was all in good fun. No one here meant harm, or would take offence.

Kate knew these people almost as well as Harold, and she knew Harold extremely well. Almost down to the latest whorl of reddish hair sprouting in his ears, the pine-tar scent of him when he'd been jogging, the sweet nature of a normally blunt man. He was a lapsed Scot, he always said. With no offended clan to speak of and no kilt to wear at family occasions. No plaintive pipes to blow. If sometimes he seemed standoffish or gruff in nature, he was more bluff than bite.

Someone was staring out the dark picture window and asked, "Hey, who moved in there, anyway?" Lights were springing on in the house across the street.

"Some lunatic," Harold said promptly.

"What, are you having trouble with rampaging dogs or loud rap music already?"

"No, not that sort of thing," Harold said, because Kate had given him a thoughtful look. As in, it was Christmas and everyone on earth should be kind. That sort of look.

"He's just a bit odd," Kate said, to help Harold out. "Performs peculiar rituals."

"A devil-worshipper? A sacrificer of small children?" Nicole stammered out. She was always so dark right off the bat. She worked in the film industry, set design for schlocky horror flicks, so it made sense.

"Not as far as we can tell. But the other day he was out there in broad daylight, as broad as it gets at this time of year, and raking his lawn," Harold said, as though that should be the clincher.

"Maybe he's an avid gardener," Cam offered. Cam was always pruning and planting the right bulbs at the right time in properly turned soil.

"No, Cam, no. You don't get it. This was a couple of days ago, right? He was raking the snow," Harold said. "Are you getting a picture here? Raking the snow."

Cam considered for a moment what sort of late-season gardening chore this might be, and then smiled. "Okay, that's weird, I'll admit."

"Maybe he has OCD," Cheryl offered. She was a psychiatric nurse, and neuroses always came first to her mind. Most people aren't serial killers, she liked to point out, just nervous as hell, with bad families, bad habits and bad attitudes.

"You know, obsessing? Like what you're doing about the fellow across the street?" Kate was clearly getting ready to end the subject.

"I think we should stop analyzing the poor guy," Linda said.

Her husband, Randy, nodded and brushed cracker crumbs from his beard. "And get over there and really find out what makes him tick."

Everyone laughed. They had gathered in a semicircle around the window and were staring out beyond the snow-lined street to the newly occupied house.

"No, seriously. Why don't we offer him some food? Invite him over?"

"It's the neighbourly thing to do," Cam said. He was what Kate's father used to call a good egg.

"Okay," Kate said, taking charge, "here's what we'll do. I'll take him a plate of goodies, a gesture of welcome. And then ask him if he'd like to join us. That way he has a choice, doesn't feel pressured. Can just shut the door in my face if he wants to and continue on with his—"

"Indoor raking," Harold said, ducking his head in a fake-ashamed way.

"You're terrible," Kate said.

She was already arranging smoked salmon and pasta salad, cheese and crackers on a plate. Covering it with saran wrap and heading out the door, with a scarf around her head and just a sweater, nothing more.

Harold watched her footsteps leave neat prints down the shovelled sidewalk newly dusted with snow. Her feet were small and pointed slightly outward, like a ballet dancer's. He hoped the guy wasn't a psycho or something.

Kate rang the bell and there was a hovering shadow in the light behind the glass transoms on either side of the door. A tallish man appeared then, bending toward her as if he might be hard of hearing.

Harold could see her small shoulders bob up and down as she spoke and then pointed across the street to their party. The man accepted the plate of food; when Kate turned to wave goodbye, the door had already closed.

"It was obvious he was shy," Kate said, shaking a few sprinkles of snow from her shoulders. "A little overwhelmed."

"Yeah, we're such a kind bunch," Nicole whispered. "Don't let it out of the bag."

"Does he have anyone living with him? A significant other?" Gretchen asked. She was once again between relationships.

"Well, the house—at least what I could see of it, front hall open to the living room—had that sort of unlived-in aspect when a man lives alone and doesn't have the faintest about hanging a painting or placing a chair," Kate said.

The subject of the new guy on the block had almost fizzled when Harold blurted out, "So did you slip in a little hint about raking his yard, what he was doing the other day?" He was clearly still bent out of shape about that, had to know.

"Well, actually I did ask him whether he'd lost something. Mentioned that we'd seen him—looking—in the front yard."

"Well, what did he say?" Harold asked. As if the explanation had to be good or else he just wouldn't buy it.

"He said he was looking for his dog's Frisbee," she said. A smile was playing around her mouth, as though she were admitting Harold had been right. The guy might be kind of loopy.

"His dog's Frisbee?" The room sprang, like a coiled cat just waiting to pounce, into sharp laughter.

They moved on to other topics. Business, the new shopping mall down the highway, recipes for Christmas desserts using champagne and fruit in tall, fluted glasses. "Sort of like a float," Linda said. "With raspberry sherbet, sliced kiwis on top. Yum."

But Harold wasn't happy. He was still thinking about the stranger across the way who now had a plate of food, offered by his wife's hands. Carried there in good faith. For as many weeks as the man had lived across the street, Harold had never once seen a dog. Not a sign of one. No barking, no chasing after thrown fetch toys. He very much doubted whether the man even had a dog. Whether he had told the truth. That bothered Harold. That bothered Harold a lot.

* * * * *

Harold was still ticked off a few days later when he went across the street, allegedly to talk shop. The fellow was fiddling with some sort of mid-sized car, an older model, maybe eighties. It was beginning to rust around the wheel wells.

The guy was wearing that trench coat again, like some sort of child molester or laid-off detective. Only pretending to work on his car, the hood raised at a suspicious angle. Not really up, not really down.

Harold shook the man's hand. He said his name was Walter Bagin. "An old Welsh name," he added, when Harold arched an eyebrow. As though even the name might be made up.

Walter's hand was dry and seemed frail for such a tall man. Then Harold couldn't help himself any longer. "So, did you ever find your dog's Frisbee?" he asked. "Or for that matter, your dog?"

Walter looked startled. Frowned and swallowed a couple of times like a baby starling getting too big a mouthful. "My dog is dead," he said finally. "My dog died," he repeated.

Harold's first reaction was to think how sly a man this must be. To invent something like that so quickly. Harold could never do that, so he had to admire the guy a little. Had to give him credit.

"Sorry about that," Harold said. He didn't sound very sorry, or feel it either. "How'd he die?" He wasn't letting him off the hook so easily. No sir.

A painful look had fallen on Walter's face. "It was a slow death. Gruesome, really," he said. Then added, "So you're a dog lover then?"

That was the first inkling Harold had that the man might be telling some sort of half-truth. And that he, Harold, might look a little shamefaced. Harold had never liked dogs and didn't want to say so. So he flinched and said, "Yeah, I like dogs. They're real people. Good companions."

"Exactly," Walter said, dropping his head again into his Chevy-something engine. But Harold could see he didn't have a clue what he was looking for. Was aimlessly pulling at wires and polishing his battery connections.

Harold would have stayed to help the poor fellow, but he couldn't handle the heavy weight that had fallen like a big wrench into the mood of tinkering with the car. When Walter had raised his head again, there had been a tear in his eye. A real tear. And he said, "I'm just trying to keep busy. You know, grieving."

Harold didn't know how a grown man could be so torn apart about losing a dog. And then admit it to a virtual stranger. Well, he was an oddball all right, just as Harold had thought all along.

* * * * *

When Harold told Kate, she looked concerned. "That's sad," she said. He had almost forgotten that women liked that sort of thing, men displaying their feelings. Men acting more like women. Because that's what it amounted to, didn't it? Men like some sort of mirror image of the female agenda, of women letting things fly out of them. Feelings, intuitions, regrets. Hurts, hatreds. So he just shrugged off her look of motherly or sisterly concern, whatever it was that skittered over her slightly freckled face. He could picture her bringing Walter some comfort food. Maybe mashed potatoes with nutmeg, plates and plates of it, while Walter wallowed and waited for Kate to arrive at his door.

That's exactly what Kate did, for eight days and eight nights, as though she had Walter on a feeding schedule like an infant.

She was "checking in on Walter," is what she said, before she almost tiptoed across the street, as though she might be disturbing him.

Harold couldn't take it one more day and said so. "Is he off the bottle yet?" he asked sullenly. "Taking solid foods?"

Kate looked astonished. If there was such a thing as "pleasantly surprised," this was a case of "unpleasantly." She looked plainly disappointed. It was the flip side of her amazement when he'd given her the engagement ring, years ago. She had looked almost *too surprised*, he had thought then. As though she hadn't really believed in the gesture, or at least not coming from this particular man. Maybe she'd wanted to make Harold happy by acting a little over-the-top, a little golly-gosh.

If he hadn't liked her astonishment then, he liked it even less now. With Walter just across the street and somehow involved. Something intimate flashed in Harold's imagining, something in half darkness, perhaps an image of Kate's breast. Walter feeding there where Harold liked to fasten on.

Kate felt it too. The tugging between them. She sensed Harold's envy. It seemed to her an almost childish fear, the way little ones liked to hang on and make a fuss. She wondered whether to laugh, but thought that might belittle the serious thing cropping up between them. She had never seen Harold act like this, overly attached to her, or, despite his blunt outbursts, seem mean-spirited.

"You don't like Walter, I gather," she said finally.

"I just don't know why you're treating him like a child," Harold said.

"When *you* want to be the child?" Kate snapped. She thought he was pouting.

Harold only sounded more exasperated. "Okay then, like some long-lost hero. Brother or father returned from the war, or Olympic champion. Why don't you build him a shrine for his so-called suffering? Made of mashed potatoes. And chicken soup."

A shrine made of chicken soup should have made them laugh. But it didn't.

That evening Kate stayed longer than usual at Walter's house. Harold tried not to care. Tried not to count the minutes passing, one by one, between 6:15 and 7:45.

"I left your supper in the warming oven," Kate said breezily, when she finally shut the front door hard, as though keeping out a strong wind. "Didn't you find it?"

Harold was shocked. She had eaten dinner with Walter. Had left Harold's plate in the oven.

* * * * *

"Do you even know what kind of dog Walter had? Do you?"

They were lying like Egyptian mummies side by side, perfectly sealed up. Trying to stay intact and not crumble to dust.

"Maybe a miniature schnauzer," she said. And sighed conspicuously, as if she were not only tired, but tired of Harold to boot.

"A what?"

"A serious little soldier of a dog," Kate said, in a curt tone. "Or maybe a blond, happy-go-lucky retriever. Always in the water, with that wet-dog smell."

Something in Harold snapped shut. She could hear it. She lay in the darkness long after his snoring had started, dreaming up types of dogs. Short-legged ones and spaniels with floppy ears, stoic French bulldogs with bulging eyes, giant mastiffs lying about the hearth, Maltese lapdogs always so effervescent, and churlish terriers with lots of spring to their step.

She hadn't the faintest idea what kind of dog Walter had loved and lost. It had been his wife's dog, that's all she knew. Some sort of fancy pedigreed dog or just a plain faithful mutt that had seemed like the last remaining piece of his wife. Walter had said so in the cluttered small kitchen.

"Like a rib," he'd said. "You can see the ribs of a sick woman you love. And after a while, that's all you can see, the rise and fall of her ribs. Still breathing, you think. Still alive."

His wife had liked the dog on the bed in the mornings—only to greet them, not to sleep there. But he had never allowed it, he confessed. Too many hairs. And the dog would try to squeeze between them, of course.

And then when she got ill, he hadn't allowed it either. She seemed too fragile and the nurse was always trying to keep things clean. But now he wished he had let the dog on the bed. Now he had regrets.

She had died of cancer, Walter told Kate. And that's when he had sold the old house and moved. Of course he had brought the dog along. Wanted to start letting it sleep wherever the heck it wanted to hunker down. Wanted to make it up to his wife.

The dog had been hit by a car the first night in the new house, he said. The gate to the yard didn't close properly, and the poor thing had probably been confused. First losing a person, then a house. Had probably gone looking for anything familiar. The dog was still alive, whining, when Walter had found the poor beast, its back grotesquely twisted. The driver had just left him there.

Walter had been steeping tea for about twenty minutes, speaking slowly and prodding the tea bag with a spoon now and again. Kate took over.

"Had your wife been sick long?" she asked. She knew that's what Walter really wanted to talk about, not the dog.

Walter had visibly slumped. "It started with a lump in her neck," he said finally. "Then they found a tumour—in her brain. It was terrible, the pain she endured."

He had tried to bury the dog in the backyard, he said, but the ground was too frozen. He had felt so helpless.

Kate took Walter in her arms while he sobbed wet gurgles on her shoulder.

She tried to imagine Harold losing her to something unseen between them. Something grown huge seemingly overnight.

* * * * *

The next morning Harold seemed in better spirits. Said maybe Walter might like to play cards sometime. Join his lackadaisical poker group. "It's not like we're cutthroat or anything. We don't exactly play hard. Or for keeps."

"It's a thought," Kate said. She looked kind of vague and pale, as though she hadn't slept well. "I don't think Walter can afford to lose much more right now. Not the shirt off his back, that's for sure."

Harold looked pleased that a truce might be rearing its tired head between them. He pulled Kate close and wrapped his arms around her small form, which resisted him somewhat—he could feel it.

From somewhere in the middle of them both, Kate's muffled voice said, "I want a dog. How 'bout we get a dog?" She sounded wary and edgy, didn't want Harold to refuse her this one thing.

He hated to admit it, but he'd been thinking along the same

lines. Of getting a dog. But first they had to decide what kind, and who would do all the walking and picking up of messes. An elegant greyhound, perhaps, or black and white spaniel? It had to have a little cachet, he said, look good while getting underfoot.

Kate was laughing now, he could feel her ribs inflate and then ease, like small bellows inside his hands. He supposed it would be mainly Kate's dog. That she would want it on the foot of the bed or asleep with her on the couch some nights. He guessed he wouldn't mind.

GARAGE SALE

There were always the early birds, thinking themselves smarter than the rest.

"Control freaks of an odd sort," Sandi remarked. She was looking down from the kitchen window to several cars parked by the curb. She hadn't priced some of the stuff yet and had no intention of lifting the garage door until she was good and ready.

"They have their different strategies, too, I've noticed," Ben added. "Some go for the big stuff—tables, stereos—almost on the run, and others prowl through the unlikeliest small castoffs, buttons and cufflinks, bathroom stoppers, running everything through their fingers, as though panning for gold."

He was thinking about the early days of their marriage, when they would go scrounging through the neighbourhood looking for cheap furniture and end up coming home with absurd mementoes: a shoe tree, maple, size twelve EE, or a lopsided lamp with a Lassie dog at its base, tongue lolling. For some reason those Saturday morning forays would always end in bed. More than the search itself, it was their pointed dismissal of most objects—Sandi donning an all-too-silly dress of silver sequins and Ben pooh-poohing a set of gold-plated golf clubs when he didn't know the first thing about the game—that kindled the spark of sex for them. As though they were in a posh club with only two members.

She must have read his mind, because she gave him a salty smile as she trundled off toward the doorbell's ring. "Screw them," she said over her shoulder.

"I'd like to screw you too," he said, as she waved her hand to shush him.

He watched her shake her head at the front door. Long loose blonde hair in the same haircut she'd had when they'd met at school. Now that was confidence, he thought. And she even looked good in sweats. He was a lucky man.

* * * * *

A woman with a red topknot that looked as though she'd shoved a bunch of curls into a blender was idling by the pool cues. She ran her fingers over the tips as if she might chalk one up and start shooting a few balls into the pockets.

"You play?" Ben asked amiably.

"Used to," she said in a hoarse voice, as though she might have been up all night winning at eight ball.

"They're a good brand," Ben said. "A real bargain for the pool shark in your family."

"I know," she said, looking at him intently. "I bought a set just like this one for an old boyfriend once."

Oops, he thought, and turned away. He wasn't touching that one with a ten-foot pole. Maybe disgruntled people went to garage sales just as much as the deliriously happy second-hand shoppers he and Sandi had once been.

The redhead hovered at the bookcase, thumbing through a few classics they'd decided to ditch.

"Thomas Hardy, I've had it with him," Sandi had said at breakfast. "All those coincidences, all that bumph about intended fate."

"What, you don't believe in true love?" he'd said, just to poke fun.

"Love, yes, but we find each other, don't you think? We don't get run over by a guy on a horse and then swoon into his arms. I mean, what are the odds?"

"It was the best of times, it was the worst of times," Ben had squawked in a fake Brit accent.

"That's Dickens, you ass," she'd said, giving him a kiss on the cheek.

"Are you moving out, or in?" the redhead asked, without looking up from *Tess of the d'Urbervilles.*

"Neither," Ben said. "We're just shifting a few things from here to there." He straightened an old bevelled mirror that was threatening to fall, its aged silvering bound to mar any likeness. "My wife has a rule of thumb; if we haven't looked at it in two years it must be time to revamp."

"But wasn't this house for sale not long ago? I remember thinking I wanted to look at it, and then suddenly it was sold. Or am I thinking of another?"

"Oh no, that was us. But that was almost three years ago—it's strange to think a whole whack of time has been eclipsed, just like that."

"My name's Moira," she said, as if her name suddenly mattered.

"Is that Moira with a *y* or an *i*?" he wondered aloud. "I think the only Moira I ever knew was a girl with long braids in kindergarten."

"With an *i*," she said, looking at him with a sudden intensity. "I haven't changed my name."

"Well, Moira with an *i*, glad to meet you." He could see Sandi giving him a questioning look. "I have to run along now and deal with the hagglers."

But the redhead kept at his heels. Lingered.

"Well, I hope this doesn't seem weird, but would you mind if I took a quick peek upstairs? I always wanted to see the layout; you can't really tell from those wide-angle shots the realtors plop into the ads, all the lights in the house blazing like the place is on a movie set."

He had to laugh at her dramatic way of putting things. At her odd request.

"Oh sure, why not," he said. "I have to go up and grab another coffee anyway."

They went upstairs, he leading the way, she humming a little toneless ditty under her breath. They had cleaned up in case anyone wanted to see the dining table and chairs. Staging and all that. A vase of fresh flowers, wine glasses clustered as if in readiness for a celebration.

"I can see you've put your personal touches on everything," she said. She was eyeing some of Sandi's paintings of the rocky shore not far off. "None of that love-peace hoopla people put on hearths nowadays, as though they don't have an original thought. My favourites are the sort of dollar-store mantras like *Dare to Dream* or *Imagine*, as if we can get to happiness by way of such chintzy advice."

He had to laugh again; she was quite the character.

"Hey, mind if I use the loo? Too much caffeine this morning, or maybe I'm preggo, ha, that would be a laugh at my age."

"No, go right ahead," he said, reluctantly. He was getting itchy to go back downstairs in case Sandi needed help. The redhead was starting to get on his nerves.

She took forever, flushed once, then again. Beneath the sound of gurgling water in the pipes, he thought he could hear a drawer being opened and closed. Then there was sniffling, and it grew louder. Out-and-out crying.

"Everything okay in there?" Ben asked.

"You don't remember me, do you?" a voice whispered, as though her tearful face might be pressed right to the door.

"What? Remember you?"

"You bloody well lived with Moira with an *i*," she said tersely. "We listened to Beethoven's 'Ode to Joy'—stared out at the stars after fucking our brains out. You gave me a plastic Mr. Peanut ring, said we would last a lifetime. You don't remember that?"

* * * * *

"She vanished into the bathroom and wouldn't come out," he murmured to Sandi. "That's what took me so long. Some sorrow about an old beau or something."

"Who? What?"

"The redhead, she's kooky as all get-out."

"We shouldn't open our house to strangers," Sandi said. "Poor you. How did you talk her out of there? At least she wasn't toting a gun or anything."

He squirmed a little when he thought of how he might best describe their back-and-forth. Set things straight. He really hadn't remembered her in the slightest. It had to be nearly twenty years ago. She looked totally different, had black hair then, he thought, and different-coloured eyes. Maybe she wore coloured contacts or something. But she'd always been bonkers, that hadn't changed. He'd actually been afraid of her.

The last stragglers were taking a few desperate board games and footstools so they wouldn't go home feeling empty-handed. Too stupid to see a real deal, or too late.

"Jesus," Ben said, as he closed the garage door. "Let's keep everything we've got and never toss out anything again."

He expected Sandi to laugh, commiserate. But she was giving him a quizzical look in the sudden dark of the lowered door.

"It's okay, you don't have to explain," she said bluntly. "Moira left a note. I went up to pee and found it stuck to the back of the bathroom door. So you two were about to get hitched—and you left her standing at the altar. No big deal," she said.

"What a load of horseshit," Ben stammered. "She was a one-night stand. Ages ago, in university. Maybe two nights, tops. And truthfully, thankfully, I can't remember a thing about it. And that's what her precious little ego is all in a knot about—that she's holding a torch for me and I never gave her a second thought."

"Well, she's coming by in a couple of days to recalibrate, as she puts it. Bringing a few mutual friends, is what she said. Just for old times' sake."

He didn't know what it meant; a friendly home invasion? They'd planned a wedding more as a joke than anything. There had never been any actual standing at any altar. They'd been drunk or stoned most of the time. He vaguely recalled a few dicey friends of hers he'd met on his way out the door. Maybe she'd go home and take her meds and feel better in the morning.

* * * * *

They jumped when the phone rang.

"I'll get it," they both said. But Sandi rose first, and faster; he felt muggy-headed, as though he might be coming down with something. They'd been sitting together, watching the new season of *Big Little Lies*, but he'd felt the tension through Sandi's arm whenever she reached for the popcorn. This garage sale wasn't leading to intimacy, he could just feel it.

"That was Moira," she said. "She wants to buy the dining table and chairs. Wanted to know how many people it'll seat with the extra bit. She's getting married, she said."

"Tell her to take a hike—she's one of those stalker types, right off the wall."

"I think it'll get rid of her," Sandi said. She'd always been so unflappable. "Let her bring her paramour along and take the damn furniture and we'll eat off the floor, plates in our laps, the way we used to. Playing house."

Sandi gave him a grin but it wasn't totally convincing.

* * * * *

They had already moved the dining set down into the garage, had no intentions of inviting the folks upstairs. The table, mahogany with a dropped apron, was heavy, a real challenge to carry down the curving stairway. They'd almost lost their grips a couple of times, Ben cursing and Sandi laughing in a slightly hysterical tone.

"No cheques," he said. "It has to be cash."

"Good point," Sandi agreed. "No bouncing, no tracking them down. That's the last thing we need."

When the van pulled up, they could see she'd brought along a couple of burly fellows. If they were old friends he couldn't recall either of them. It was hard to say which of the two might be her intended soulmate.

One of them eased his way out of the passenger seat slowly and turned a blank stare toward the house. He sported a long, thin white cane, and Moira walked beside him protectively.

"Meet Sonny," she said, with a flinty smile. "He's fearless, was a cliff diver in Mexico and hit the water at a wrong angle. So now he's legally blind; he can see shapes, shadows, but that's about it."

The other fellow, Dimitri, with his sallow complexion and narrowed eyes, dark unibrow, didn't seem full of life either. He slunk along rather than walked. They were probably both con men, could slash open a face with that fake cane, Ben thought.

He swung open the garage door, and indicated the table and chairs as the sun struggled to come out to give the lacquer a swish shine.

Moira seated herself, as if expecting coffee and croissants. As if on cue Sonny tap-tapped his way toward the table and gingerly sat down as well. His shtick was quite convincing, Ben had to admit. The Dimitri guy sat at one end of the table, glowering like a crime boss.

"I'm just sitting a bit to see how comfortable the chairs are," Moira said.

Oh no, now she was going to barter, Ben realized too late. She was smiling brightly, too brightly. Was being quite the drama queen, leaning forward, as if reaching for the baked potatoes, then leaning back, as if after an ample meal. The legally blind leading the certifiably crazy, Ben thought bleakly.

When Sandi joined them and sat across from Moira, Ben raised an eyebrow. He wanted them on their way. Ciao, see you later, alligator.

Sandi offered them a deal, said she'd take one hundred dollars off the price. As if they were owed something. And Ben scowled, clearly didn't like it.

"Something old, with a grandma vibe, and something new and surprising," mad Moira muttered. "Something borrowed, something blue…"

The table *was* old, had been in his family forever. Suddenly he regretted letting it go. Wanted to tell Moira and her pals to bugger off, forget the whole deal. But he wasn't brave enough to take up the slack.

"Here, let me carry a couple of chairs out to the street," Ben offered.

As he reached for a chair beside Sandi, Sonny whipped his long, thin metal cane across Ben's knuckles. Ben's middle finger crumpled against the chair back as Sandi rose and howled in horror.

Moira stood then and held out a curved knife, the sort used to gut fish, leaned across the table toward Sandi. Ben pulled Sandi back with his good hand, while Moira etched a long zigzag line along the table's surface, the knife blade making a terrible scritching sound. Dimitri kicked a couple of chairs to the floor to block any pursuit, the threesome hoofing it to the van, Sonny in the lead and hopping nimbly into the driver's seat, Dimitri howling with laughter like a hyena. Moira slipped into a back seat before the van squealed away from the curb, burning rubber.

* * * * *

Sandi was wrapping Ben's hand in an absent-minded fashion, holding it against the ice; it was swelling, a dark purple.

"You should probably get that looked at," she said.

"It hurts like a bugger, if that's any indication of a broken finger or two," Ben said, wincing at her touch.

"I guess that's what she wanted," Sandi said, with an edge to her voice.

Things were going to get difficult, he could see that. He would have to tell her everything, how he'd skedaddled because Moira had been off her nut, even then. Sandi would understand.

But she could probably figure out the timing. That he'd screwed Moira after meeting Sandi. That was the bad part. So maybe he'd have to keep everything between them hidden. He had to decide.

"We'll have to move," Sandi said. "I don't feel safe here anymore."

Ben could feel a dark collapse inside himself, a hollowing—she had loved this house. He knew how hard it would be to pack up and resettle. Almost impossible.

"We'll keep the table and chairs," Sandi said. "A table runner should cover the gouging, and if nothing else, it'll make a good story at dinner parties."

SUNDAY DRIVE TO GUN CLUB ROAD

At one time, when owning a car was still a big deal, and gas cheap, land even cheaper—you could buy acres of the stuff, with scrub trees and a gouged-out gravel pit, for a song—taking a drive was the classic pastime. Or so my father once told me. On Saturday, he said, it was the kids' job to wash the car for the big outing, flinging soap bubbles at one another, earning their paltry allowances. Sunday you got behind the wheel after filing out of church, pressed by something you couldn't name, as though you had to make a run for it, get somewhere and fast. If you took to the back roads all that blather about salvation that had hurt your ears while the smarmy priest droned on and on would just fly out the window, my father said. He liked to joke about things.

Long after churchgoing had fizzled—the white clapboard husk of St. Mary's on our street mainly stood hollow and empty, only a few blue-hairs straggling in to pray for people like ourselves, spiritually lost—my family still had the habit of hitting the road. It was nearly the end of a century famous for gas guzzling and wasting time between wars, but we had pent-up energy on Sundays to get going, to be somewhere.

I thought of our aimless trips along the shimmering roads as one of those wavy pencil illusions when you waggle your fingers just to impress yourself because nobody else cares. Or like some head-hurting math problem: How long will it take this family to reach any sort of destination, given a few random detours, like us nearly hitting a bear cub once, my mother shrieking, "Oh for the love of Martha!" and the grim fact that the car burned oil, constantly needed topping up? Our being together in a moving vehicle was an act of faith, one my father believed would assign us a history, save us from being unremarkable as a family. We'd go zooming down some potholed country road, in any old direction in any blunted weather, and simply stare out the windows of our old clunker Oldsmobile as if we were watching our favourite TV show, *The Passing Scenery*.

After a few hours of looking for God knows what, we'd stop somewhere, maybe at an old diner called the Hilltop or the Rendezvous, one of those places still serving real pie or big milkshakes from a noisy retro blender on the counter. And for a while that became the gambit: finding just such a homey place, with pan-fried potatoes and my father's old faves, creamed chicken on toast or fried liver with onions. Once we drove south of the line to some hole in the wall near Snohomish, Washington, but a cop pulled us over for rubbernecking, as he called it. Asked us what our business was, the state trooper not nearly as friendly as our Canadian Mountie sort. He didn't laugh when my father asked, "What, do we look like potheads?" So we stayed north of the border, looking for sudden roadside rewards, what we seemingly deserved.

It couldn't be fast food—my father had no patience for the overly sweet slop that all tasted the same. "You call this pathetic little morsel a burger?" he'd said once, the girl behind the takeout window sliding it shut on his fingers. It was part of my father's shtick to be a food critic, an everything critic. I had this odd feeling he wasn't just trying to entertain us, but to show us something that needed watching.

I noticed he never complained about my mother's cooking; she always packed a few things with a chunk of dry ice in the cooler, sandwiches with fatty deli meats, her gloppy potato salad, a few pieces of nearly spoiled fruit. In good weather we'd find a picnic spot and chow down, kick a ball about for a bit. Listen to the birds or watch someone chasing a headlong dog, trying to call it back.

I don't remember how the house thing started. More than once my father rolled down the window, took a deep breath, and spoke of getting a farm, growing our own food, that whole back-to-the-land thing where enterprising sorts could be smarter than the average joe, self-sufficient. He taunted my mother with leaving his job—but after the look of alarm on her face he left that topic alone. He'd worked for the railroad since forever, new technologies and old decrepit trains making his stints as signal man or conductor, yard master or bridge inspector ever more erratic; he'd been transferred more than promoted, that's how my mother put it. Still, he stood to get a decent pension for all the runaround. So maybe they were both thinking of the future, how it could look different when we went toodling along some gravel road north of nowhere.

I know the first time we wandered into one of those public showings of houses that needed selling—and fast—we were hooked. By the risky notion, perhaps, of people's hopes so exposed. As if someone might buy six rooms and a specialty koi pond or flagstoned breezeway on impulse. Or maybe with a vengeance, like a drive-by shooting. Something simmering in the back of their minds, a kind of reckoning.

We'd scoff and roll our eyes at the so-called staging of rooms, the frayed and faded objects that might describe a particular family tucked away in cupboards while flowers swayed in vases, kitschy plaques saying *There's No Place Like Home* or *Be Free as a Bird* hung over a scorched fireplace that had stopped burning wood eons ago.

"Those signs are majorly annoying," my sister Amy piped up after we'd had our fill of crescent-shaped moons in bedrooms promising *Sweet Dreams* or paddle-shaped folksy art saying *Beach* when we were nowhere near water, or even worse, when we were—the house on a jutting cliff with no way down to the Pacific rolling in below. "Sweatshop-made by kids barely old enough to go to school in some burb in Bangkok or Shanghai. And they *don't*—go to school, I mean. They just make shit like that for rich people to close deals on houses. It makes me sick."

She was going through her idealistic, clean-up-her-act phase. But my mother told her she shouldn't swear in front of my younger brother, a gnarly eleven-year-old stuck between his sisters in the back seat, reading crime comics and laughing giddily at some murder gone wrong.

To my mind, the near-empty, freshly scented rooms with lavender-painted walls without scuff marks or cobwebs in the corners looked hokey, sure, and you'd hit your shins on the glass coffee tables if you actually lived there. But the fake-fancy stuff wasn't nearly as depressing as the cluttered houses: tons of grandchildren's photos and knitted dealies over every chair, obviously the hangout of old folks about to move into rest homes. Or maybe even keeled over, suddenly dead and gone. It made me sad to think the knick-knacks might be all that remained of their lives, ceramic cock-a-doodle doodads for holding spoons, amber glass ashtrays from when it was still cool to smoke indoors and give your newborn a stroke from all the fumes.

My sister Amy was good to have along on these outings, because she was more and more obviously expecting. Her soccer-ball tummy with its pierced belly button poking out of her shortie T-shirts made people think we were serious, maybe even desperate, about this house-buying business. Not just kicking tires.

My dad laughingly called her condition "knocked up," despite my mother frowning and saying it wasn't polite—or even respectful—to Amy. She said it as though good manners and leaving someone to make their own mistakes were two different notions.

"It used to mean woken up, someone banging on the shutters to get you out of bed, back in Shakespeare's day," my father replied. "And in that sense I would say Amy is well and truly knocked up."

He chortled again, because he always found himself amusing. And expected us to be onside, or else he got hurt feelings like a big kid. So my mother's tight laugh, just to keep him company, often started ahead of the punchline. She was an appeaser, if not an outright enabler. Hitler might have been worse if she'd been his mother.

"Who'd live on Gun Club Road?" my father protested after we'd traipsed around a living room with lumpy wall-to-wall carpet browning at the edges, and bedrooms with no sheets on the beds. Just bare mattresses. As if the name of the road had made someone move out in a big hurry. Monster truck repossessed, and the deadbeat renters walking a fine line between petty theft and real crime.

"Yes, that one's definitely out," my mother agreed, as if they were actually discussing the pros and cons of the neighbourhood.

There was another open house just one street over, on Marble Road.

"I have a hunch that old crook of a realtor is a hard-core closer on deals with leaking basements and parasites under the laminate flooring," my dad said when we left the place with complacent smiles on our faces and headed to our ages-old dinosaur of a car. I mean, the car alone should have given us away.

"Too Italian," my mother said of the kitchen, "and I don't get the big shift toward granite counters. They stain like crazy, red wine, fruit juices, you name it. Besides, I don't like my kitchen to be too show-offy."

"Yeah, the place was a little over-the-top," I agreed. "As if a cheap rancher can look like a villa near Rome. More like the fall of Rome. Ha ha!" I was starting to sound like my joke-a-minute father. Trying too hard.

There was a front-seat discussion then about where the best granite came from, whether from eastern Canada, Quebec, my mother thought, or some quarry in India or Brazil, my father countered, where they don't have to deal with the environmental rigmarole. "The poor souls mining the stuff die of lung diseases from all the dust," my father added, as if he were suddenly the greenest guy on earth.

"Who was it that said luxury should feel like comfort?" my mother asked, waggling her head around in small circles, as though her neck might be kinked by all of our far-fetched travels.

"Coco Chanel," my sister offered. "And it must have been an afterthought, 'cause she had a shitty life, despite all the parties on the Riviera and the glitzy jewels. Never found her happy place."

It was something Amy had read in her fashion mags, no doubt.

I could see my mother wanted to curb Amy's blunt language again, but she changed the shape of her mouth and her mind along with it, suddenly admitted she was uncomfortable with *this whole thing*.

"What whole thing?" my father asked.

"Taking our shoes off and tiptoeing around people's private spaces. As if we were looking in on their lives and finding them lacking. Judging books by their covers, so to speak."

My mother was master of the blurt, saying something offhand that was really a warning in disguise. It was the only way she could get anyone's attention. As if she'd said something important by accident, and never mind her.

"What—you think we should leave our shoes on?" my father said, trying for a laugh.

"No," my mother said. That was all. But there was a sparking in the air, like when you forget to rip off the foil before putting an instant dinner in the microwave.

"Well, the notion of an open house," my father continued, "is clearly an invitation." He could feel the sting of her reproach, no matter how slight. "These wiseass realtors are daring folks to be enthralled about the rotten wiring in the basement or the deck that needed replacing years ago. I can't believe some of these places and the prices they want. The realtor always saying he'll have to check on the actual bona fide lot line, or that we can add on in the future, when he's just BS'ing us. It takes a certain nerve—so we shouldn't feel bad. Far from it," he added, just so we all got the point.

But my mother didn't quit. I had to admire her sudden show of spunk.

"The last realtor was a woman," she said quietly, "who answered your questions quite handily, I thought." My mother was clearly doing some daring of her own.

My father said nothing more, just firmed up something in his jaw and kept his eyes on the road.

I wanted to fix it between them, agree with my mother's old-fashioned common sense and still run with my father's bluster. I have to admit I liked looking at other people's updated bathrooms, with their little baskets of different coloured soaps, or their so-called great rooms, with faux-leather couches and rugs sporting the bright colours of a cheap trip to Mexico. The gas fireplaces with fake logs lighting up at the press of a button, the spacious sofas with oodles of throw cushions at just the right angles, not too heaped in a pile and not too scattered. I felt relieved to see houses that shiny and polished, like a neat ending to a story, not like our house, always under construction with one of my father's notions to expand the front porch to something bigger than a welcome mat, or to make the extra room in the basement into a separate suite for Amy's incoming squawker. As far as I knew my father liked tearing things down, not so much building them up again.

Every now and then we would find a few upscale places in our searches, in recently tree-shorn neighbourhoods called Eagle's Watch or Bonnybrook Place, the homes bigger and newer, more costly and out of reach. My father was getting ideas on the road, he would say to us. "Of what *not* to do, hardy har har. Like those fake mullioned windows, with their chintzy little plastic inserts? Give me a break."

"That's good," my mother said, humouring him again, as though what had briefly reared up between them was settled. It felt endless, relentless, as if we would always pile into the old Cutlass on Sundays and look for a promising aspect to the landscape, a house perched on a knoll as though it belonged, something that would make us stop, take our shoes off, tread lightly in the sacred spaces of other lives. Then turn around and go home to our so-called character house of cracked stucco with fake Georgian mansion pillars, the furniture all mismatched hand-me-downs, every room crammed with failed intention to sort or paint, to feel less dissatisfied.

On one of our Sunday jaunts an elderly couple took a particular shine to our whimsical family, in which we all played our parts. My brother, when he got tired or hungry, started acting half his age. Six at best, all whiny and crumpled. So at the umpteenth house of that day's touring—"it is a gracious house, with good bones," the realtor insisted—my brother said aloud, in a hectic voice, "Why aren't there ever more people at these things? I don't get it. Why are we the only ones?"

My father took him aside and said just as loudly, in his typical swashbuckling style, "You know, son, at an open house down near Dallas, Texas, way back in 1952, they offered free Dr. Pepper soft drinks to all comers, and a Cadillac to the lucky buyer of any brand-spanking-new house in the suburbs they were building. And you know how many people showed up? Thirty thousand. Thirty *thousand*. Now *that* was hoopla!"

My brother was looking blank and his stomach was gurgling. The owners of the house—they hadn't vamoosed, like you're supposed to—brought out a plate of tired Oreos. I swear there was dust on the cookies. But my brother dove in.

They were a sad-faced look-alike pair, like John and Yoko, as if people found a certain sameness in a face made them feel more at home with a stranger. Or how people come to look like their droopy-jowled dogs, so maybe this pair had once had a hound or something. All I know is that they *hovered*, that was the only word for it. Seemed to be assessing the possibilities as we moved from room to room in our stockinged feet and poked at window ledges, flipped light switches on and off.

And they told us things, private things not generally admitted to prospective buyers. How a baby had died in the house in the early years. And how the house itself, with its grand old front porch and radiators hissing in every room, had seemed to shore them up, give them the constitution required to carry on. They'd never had another child—had lost their nerve, so to speak. But the creaking staircases and Victorian gables housing the memories of the child had seemed enough to care for, to inhabit.

"That's why it's never been on the market, up for grabs. But since my husband's stroke, well, he needs so many visits to the hospital, we've decided to move close by, have an apartment for the time being. I mean, enough time has passed, it feels as though someone else could care for… our Jimmy," the woman said, her sparse hair permed to a frizz that made her seem fraught, still.

The realtor, who'd been pacing in another room, clearly chagrined with the off-the-rails sellers, had finally broken things off with a spiel about new soffits and a dandy energy-saving gas furnace about to be installed.

"Whoa," my dad said, when we hit the car. "That was some sales pitch. And it never seemed to occur to them that Amy is—in the family way," he said, gloating at my mother with his eloquent language, "and might not want to hear that sort of thing."

"People in their grief," my mother muttered.

"I would like to know how the dead baby got that way. I mean, dead," my brother the private detective said, now that his blood sugar was restored.

"What, you think arsenic in his mashed peas? Or maybe they locked him in a toy box for using bad words until he turned blue in the face?" I asked, trying to pique my brother into acting normal for once.

"They didn't say his age," my mother broke in, tartly. As if we were finally, after all these years, getting on her nerves. "But he was a baby, they said, so too young to speak much at all."

Our surmising of rusted swing sets and choking on food grew disinterested by the time we reached the next open house with blue balloons swinging merrily from a tree branch, a windswept sign promising *Free Coffee!*

"That's made up my mind already," my father said, giving way to his usual mirth. "Yum, yum. Something on the hot plate since early Jurassic times."

The winding pathway to the house had the sweet smell of rotting pine needles and twisted tree roots all set to trip you up.

"This entrance doesn't lend itself to bringing in the groceries," my sister said. She was starting to sound eerily like a mother, all warning and worry.

And then she suddenly doubled up, made an argh groaning sound, as though someone had just stabbed her in the stomach. She straightened up again, her eyes tearing.

"Wow, that was a doozer," she stammered. "A burning flash in baby town—as if I just swallowed a shot of brandy on the tip of a knife."

She had some potential as a writer, I thought just then. It would be something to kill time while she breastfed. And breastfed.

My father took her by the elbow. As though he would gladly walk her down the aisle if only he could find any reputable young man my sister had never yet met.

I had to wonder how many shots of brandy my sister, at sweet seventeen, had swallowed. And with whom? The mystery father? She'd never said who it was, had just burst into tears of rage—it looked like to me—every time the subject came up. Boys of high school–dropout age didn't usually tipple brandy in snifters. So someone of my father's ripe old vintage? The thought gave me a coy twisting of innards. As though I could feel the kid inside my sister wiggling, insisting the truth come out in a big sloppy plop.

The house didn't have an easy flow, my father said, pointing to a long dark corridor branching off to a series of small, shadowy rooms.

The realtor was young, full of ideas. "Yeah, I agree. You could knock down a few walls and really open up the space." He smelled of nervous sweat and sprucing up with cologne and my sister started to look a little green in the face.

"We're going outside for a spell," my mother said. "Fresh air."

I could see them through what the realtor called the retro picture window in the low-ceilinged living room. And the picture wasn't pretty. My sister was throwing up in the rock garden, splashing the plants with her plumes of roadside picnic lunch. Always too much salt and mayo, you could count on it with my mother, no matter what the menu.

As distraction, my father led the young fellow toward the kitchen, which smelled of mould and fake-lemon cleaning agents. "So what about drainage?" he asked, looking up the sloping backyard to the neighbours' back fence looming above, as though the house being pitched as a mid-century, cute-as-a-bug rancher might lie in a gulch or river bottom.

I gave my dad the high sign when my sister had disappeared back toward the car, holding tight to my mother's arm.

We went out the back way, so the realtor my father later called a shifty-eyed young grifter wouldn't see my sister's display over the hydrangeas. Or smell it.

"Ah, a carport," my father said. "A notion from gentler times."

I knew what he meant, though the realtor looked stymied. I'd once asked my father why garages were the first thing you saw with so many newer houses. And he'd scoffed, as if he couldn't believe the way the world was heading, and said "security," so people could go straight from their locked cars into their locked houses, no fuss, no muss with someone skulking around. I realized I'd been at risk my whole life, getting off my bike in plain view and entering the house by the side door.

"Well, thanks so much," my father said, shaking the realtor's sweaty hand. "Sorry we don't have time for the coffee. We're late for a showing."

"Oh, oh... here's my card," the jumpy guy offered. "Barry—if you have any questions."

My father put the car into high gear, spurting gravel as we departed.

"Feeling any better?" he asked into the rear-view mirror.

"Not much," my sister murmured. Her face was a ghastly grey, with none of that peachy motherly glow.

"I think it's a sign," my mother said, looking directly at my father's right ear.

"That we should skedaddle home? Call it a day?"

"That we should stop doing this—dropping in on a whim. When we have no intention of ever buying any of these… places."

She seemed to be blaming him for something, but I couldn't tell exactly what. A lurid affair came to mind, the kind of secret dalliance that would rear up in the movies and bust a family wide open. But it would have to be a woman as generous as my mother in laughing at bad jokes. And doing it naked, which was highly unlikely.

Everyone in the car went silent, felt strangely alone in a crowded Oldsmobile smelling ever so faintly of throw-up. My sister was slumping toward the window, pressing her cheek against the glass, the passing scene suddenly struck with bleary spatters of rain.

My brother was cracking his knuckles loudly and making that growly sound in his throat he does when he's trying to stem one of his stupid questions.

"But what would we do—I mean, on Sundays?" He couldn't help himself.

My father sighed a long flubber of an out-breath, sounding like a snorting horse. He seemed to be at a loss for words, which surprised me. He couldn't exactly spell it out, he finally said, how the trips we'd taken were an investment of sorts, in a common vision. But he seemed to be hinting at the fact that we might otherwise be in trouble as a family, might all go our separate ways if not for our playful considerations of this mud room or that in-law suite. He seemed to be saying that our sightseeing ritual was our church without the church, our roadside redemption.

That was when I noticed the bright stain seeping out from beneath my sister.

"Shit," I croaked out. "Amy's bleeding all over the seat!" Her head was bumping against the glass by now and she didn't seem to care.

My father did an about-turn and drove like a crazy man toward the hospital only a few minutes to the south. He blared his horn at red lights, green lights and intersections with no lights at all, and gestured with his hands off the wheel at dithering pedestrians, my mother with her head out the window, screaming, "We've got to get to the hospital! Get out of the damn way!"

I'd never heard her swear before so I knew this was serious.

They took Amy on a stretcher straight from the car, while my clueless brother thought to note aloud that it was just like an ER drama on TV, except in real life. My mother gave him a horrified look, as if to say, "Whose child are you?" So he clammed up while my father paced in the waiting room. My mother tried to look at magazines, but I could see her eyes lifting and peering into the middle distance, measuring something.

Amy pulled through, of course she did. She's a tough cookie, as my father would say, which doesn't always sound like a compliment. But the poor little jelly mold of a baby didn't make it. It pissed me off, because I'd already spent nights and nights, while falling asleep, trying to name the kid I would probably be babysitting.

And I kept revisiting those houses we'd looked at and talked about. They came back to me, one by one, in that near-dream state when your mind whirls with possibilities. The family room in a big so-called cottage, with a stone fireplace, the wood stacked neatly beside, ready for flaming. The kitchen nook in another, with its bench seating, like a picnic mood dragged inside. The teensy view of the ocean beyond, its glimmer of light through a dark fringing of woods.

We no longer take Sunday drives, it's true. But we bought a house, a real beaut of an old-timer with hardwood floors and fancy coved ceilings. The one with the dead baby. It has a great backyard with stately old trees where I hang suspended in the saggy old hammock my father strung up. And now, as a family joke, we call Amy's sad day her Jimmy. Use that day as a marker, to hold our places. Although it's not a name I would have chosen.

EX-RACEHORSES

When she went to their house for dinner, she brought along a bag of corn, a dozen sweet peaches and cream, and a small book of poetry with the title *Blown Kisses*. She was nervous and couldn't think of anything else.

The corn was fresh out of the fields among the dairy farms east of the city. It was the kind of food that put everything out in the open. You could see right away who used too much butter, who ate the corn in a neat row before turning the corncob round or might take random bites with no pattern at all. Or who might be fussy enough to pick away at the niblets with a fork. And you could tell a lot about a person by the cooking of corn. Some people still boiled it to death, like at a church picnic, while others steamed it gently over the inside leaves, were more careful.

Leigh didn't read poems, but a friend had just published her first collection, swore the cherry-red lips on the cover to be her own. Way too personal, thought Leigh, who didn't like to give too much away. A book about kisses, even the sort flown from your fingers as mimed affection, seemed a little dicey. But blown kisses were once sent to the gods, little puckered prayers wishing yourself a little luck. That's what Leigh had learned from browsing through the hand-bound chapbook. And you taught babies to blow kisses, smooch their clammy little hands to their mouths, saying bye-bye. She figured it was no more risky a gift than bringing the wrong sort of wine. Especially since Stan and his girlfriend might not be drinking anything but fruit smoothies or tall glasses of milk.

The couple already had a real live baby—had rushed headlong through any phase of testing the waters. Maybe in your forties (which Stan clearly was, and the girlfriend clearly wasn't) it all seemed urgent; you didn't pick each other apart anymore looking for right-seeming passion. You knew yourself better, and knew better than to know anyone else too well. Maybe a tiny squirming infant was proof of a sacrifice that Leigh had never yet made.

Leigh (named by her mother after a film star best known as a girl slashed to pieces in a Hitchcock movie) thought the whole thing with Stan and the baby was a little quirky, but then she'd done a few rash things, too. Unlike her mother, who loved the pretend aspects of marriage and movie stars equally—you learned your role and gave it your all—Leigh kept coming up short in any attempt to take love seriously.

It was she who had drifted from the marriage, not the other way around. They'd fought about having kids once too often and she'd flown off the handle. Was a bit of a redhead, Stan had said, although she had only a touch of red in her long chestnut ponytail and he'd probably meant hothead. She'd thought her running away might whet their appetites for a different sort of life, Stan a struggling musician and still wanting kids; she'd be stuck at home while he went on tour with his band of rockabilly pals who all had affairs on the road—it was common enough.

She'd ended up going to Austin, Texas, of all places, just to bother Stan—he'd always wanted to hit the city's live music scene, dozens of places to strut your stuff. Her fling with an architect was short-lived; he loved to hear the sound of his own voice, drew his upscale rancheroo designs on cloth napkins in high-end restaurants and then offered to sell them as a kind of self-promoting stunt. The whole thing had left her feeling slightly abused. And for Stan it was even worse.

She'd taken for granted that Stan would forgive her, take her back when she was ready. Even somewhat ready to change her mind about having children. And then it had just been too late. He'd been badly wounded, which she hadn't foreseen, had met someone else.

All the men since Stan had clearly been bad choices and then worse. She'd gone out with a stunt rider for spaghetti westerns who'd wanted to rough her up, then a high roller with a coke problem; had thought a high school teacher might be a safe bet until he admitted a tendency toward getting involved with his underage students. She didn't trust herself any longer, that's what it amounted to. If she guessed a man had kind eyes he was bound to be holding some unnatural grudge; she was that good at being wrong. She couldn't seem to fasten down on anyone worth worrying about, except as lingering regret.

Leigh thought in future she should stick to men who didn't say much, like Stan, who, apart from plucking at his guitar and singing mournfully, had been a quiet soul. It was words that tripped her up, she'd decided. All the promises and plans, the spin on real lives. She tended to believe what people said.

"What do you do?" the girlfriend asked not long into shucking the corn. She was not going to use the inner leaves of the tender ears or steam the corn gently. She was plunking it into a pot of boiling water.

Leigh could see the girlfriend had weak hands, long thin fingers used for shuffling portfolios and reassuring people about their mutual funds. Which she had done until her ninth month, she said. So her hands might also be frail from lack of sleep and lots of clenching, Leigh figured.

That's how Elke—the name was Danish—and Stan had met, puzzling over ethical investments. She'd been his advisor, though Leigh didn't remember them ever having any money to spare for an abandoned gold mine in Burkina Faso or new wind turbines along the Oregon coast. Maybe he was just planning on making a bundle from shares in a tech start-up, maybe that was it. And the bundle turned out to be in diapers.

The girlfriend didn't say anything after Leigh had said, "I train horses. Mostly ex-racehorses who need a career change after miserable lives running in circles. I remake them into show horses, mainly jumpers, or hobbies for lonely teenagers."

Leigh supposed she didn't know what to say. Was hopeless at small talk about horses. Or had been struck by the possibility of an ex-racehorse seeming somehow burnt out or cast off, like an ex-husband.

"The owners are mostly gamblers who can't pay their bills. They don't care a hoot about the horses, running their hearts out and mostly losing—they're not exactly ethical investors," Leigh explained. But the girlfriend didn't respond.

Perhaps Leigh shouldn't have added the bit about stepping in before the meat man comes around. The girlfriend didn't eat meat. It was better for the baby, she said.

She was tired, the girlfriend said, from being up at all hours during the night. And yawned then to prove it.

"I used to get up early to check the markets, thought it was a matter of taking the right risks at the right time. Now I'm frazzled about things closer to home," the girlfriend said, looking down to the wizened little Stan face scowling in one of those carryall car seats plunked by her feet. "I've come to think it's mostly luck, and we should hang on to the little bit we're given," the girlfriend muttered.

Leigh bristled, thought the girlfriend was reminding her that she'd wanted too much, hadn't been grateful. But she shrugged off the sensation of rebuke; she wasn't looking for trouble.

The girlfriend was talking out of the corner of her mouth, which looked like smiling but wasn't. This crooked half speaking was perhaps the side effect of burping a spitting baby on one shoulder. The new mother was pretty in a beleaguered way, Leigh had to admit: dark roots showing in her feathered blonde hair, slightly smudged mascara and layers of unresolved things in large green eyes. Her clothes were expensive, but mismatched and crumpled: an oversized linen shirt over drawstring been-to-Bali pants, the colours all in-between, what people called taupe-aubergine or vanilla-mocha.

But who was she to judge; Leigh hardly ever looked at herself in a mirror, scarcely wore makeup, lived in her jeans and had a tanned, lean look she could feel to be true of herself from all her work outdoors. She was still the way Stan had known her, tomboyish and younger-seeming than her midthirties, though she'd decided to wear a summery skirt for this occasion, not too clingy, just to seem discreet and careful.

Dinner wouldn't be long, the girlfriend promised, and gave the fussing child an engorged right breast to demonstrate her capabilities in keeping everyone fed. She already looked practised at this baby thing, even though this was her first. When she pressed the little tot with a reddening face into Leigh's unwilling arms, she said matter-of-factly, "Don't shake him. People always want to shake babies."

Leigh carried the baby to a window, his brow creasing at the shimmering light in the leaves of the trees beyond. She saw Stan's lanky legs braced against the porch railing; he was tipping back in his chair and sipping at a beer straight from the bottle, just the way he used to drink it, slowly and thoughtfully, savouring the bitter taste. Stan rose then, as if he sensed he was being watched. The baby was waving his arms, getting a bit frantic, so she quickly turned away from the dazzling sun, didn't want him to start bawling. She let the little guy grasp her forefinger with a fierce grip, and he seemed content then, just hanging on to someone. Piece of cake, Leigh thought. Maybe she had the makings of a mother after all.

* * * * *

Leigh went to help Stan clean up the dishes. He and Elke didn't believe in dishwashers. Too wasteful, he said, and they were trying to do their bit for the planet. Hoped that little Otto would do the same. Poor kid probably came by his name via some flak from the Danish side of the family, Leigh thought. And with a handle like that might end up being a drifter or a hard-nut CEO, she couldn't decide.

The girlfriend was sitting in the darkened dining room behind them. She was huddled with the baby and see-sawing both sides of a dialogue with a speechless, burbling infant, her voice rising and falling. That's what happens when you become a doting child amuser, Leigh thought. You coo a lot, start to sound a little off the rails.

A listless song by Emmylou Harris, who had that tragic persona common to country music, was playing from an old-time radio in the kitchen. Stan didn't write his bluesy Nashville songs any more, he said. Or play them either. He didn't have time for that stuff, he insisted, as though he'd graduated to some place more convincing than his former life. He was sticking to his old job in sales, some lighting firm that had invented a long-lasting light bulb without the mercury. "How many light bulbs does it take to change a man?" was their motto. He'd made a joke but he wasn't cracking a smile. He seemed none too excited about his prospects. Was drying each glass over and over, gingerly taking the dishes Leigh had washed from the drying rack. Each time their hands were almost touching.

He hadn't said much during dinner. But Leigh had basically read his mind. That he was afraid of something. He wouldn't really meet her eyes, the muscles in his shoulders all bunched up like a horse about to spook. Former racehorses had this startled gazing thing they did, as though seeing a shimmering spaceship on the horizon—something too hard to fathom—right before stopping dead in their tracks. Or rearing up, flying sideways.

"I was never a big fan of country music," Leigh said with a smile, to remind him. She thought it might be her way of saying Austin had been a mistake.

Then Stan started to cry. Leigh was flabbergasted, had her wrists deep in the soapy water, was struggling with the baked-on beans of a vegetable lasagna. Still, she gave him a lathery embrace; there were bubbles behind his ear when the girlfriend came into the kitchen, breathing heavily. Leigh guessed there was a quiet exertion in holding a sleeping infant in a cramped position.

The girlfriend narrowed her eyes at them. She could see Stan's bewildered look, the traces of wet matting together his long black eyelashes. He still had his lean face, the one formerly shadowed under a cowboy hat. But the hope in it had grown lined: Leigh could see how he'd aged.

The girlfriend wanted Stan to change the baby.

"But he's asleep," he stammered. Still, he took the boy carefully, his tall frame stooped a little in retreat.

Leigh turned back to the sudsy dishes, dropped her eyes away from the confusion in the room. The small uproar. Then the girlfriend dug in beside her, holding a dishtowel. The sound of wailing began in the background.

"Have you ever ridden?" Leigh asked. "Horses, I mean."

Leigh guessed it would be the proverbial dude-ranch story, some first and last time somewhere in the Cariboo or Chilcotin: the girth too loose, the rider swept off under a low-hanging branch, the horse shambling home ahead of time. The cowboys laughing, in that gritty way they had of finding fear somehow funny.

But the girlfriend surprised her. "I'd like to try it," she said. "I hear you have to be very patient. That horses are so sensitive you can bend them out of shape, just like that."

Leigh wondered if Stan had told her that.

"Yeah, that's right. They have highly developed personal bubbles, are always worrying about getting caught up in something they can't get free of," Leigh agreed. "It's hardwired into them, 'cause in the wild it's game over if they get hurt. They can't exactly hole up and get better; they have to shake a leg, move along with the bunch. That's why they're such big babies."

"Big, yes," the girlfriend said.

Then the dishes were stacked in bright piles of platters and smaller side plates, even the cups and saucers from the after-dinner coffee for Leigh, the herbal tea for the girlfriend. Everything was tidied up and clean and waiting for some next move.

Leigh said dinner had been great, though the lasagna had been burnt, the corn turned to mush. The girlfriend said Stan had obviously fallen asleep with the baby. It was true; the house was suddenly silent.

They gave one another an awkward half hug in the darkened doorway and whispered goodnight in the conspiracy of keeping the baby asleep. The cluster of surrounding houses was dark, obviously settled families who turned in early. The girlfriend had switched off the porch light before Leigh had even swung up inside her big old Chevy truck, the one she used for hauling horses. She felt uneasy, as though she had forgotten something. It was probably just the phantom feeling of holding a small volume of blown kisses and a bag of corn.

The diesel started with a chatter and roar that could wake a whole street of sleeping babies. As she pulled away Leigh felt an unreasonable anger; she knew she wouldn't see baby Stan again. That she wouldn't get a repeat invite as the boy grew into words and making his parents proud. It had been Stan's idea to invite her over—there was no reason they couldn't stay friends, he'd said. But she knew now there were reasons.

Her mind was spinning, like hot tires in a hurry to get somewhere on a summer's night. She was trying to pinpoint why it was, exactly, that Stan had spilled those sudden tears. Overtired? Too much under the thumb of the can-do girlfriend? Or because he'd lost his music? Or maybe, just maybe, he was still desperately in love with the horse-crazy girl he'd written into his first song. In Leigh's thinking, she had conceded to him—he'd been right. And now it all seemed less clear, as though Stan hadn't known his own mind when she'd counted on being wrong.

The streets were strangely deserted, as if only a few lonely stragglers were chasing through the dark for answers. Leigh drove with reckless speed, the intersections all seemingly turned the wrong way, bright-green arrows pointing her in a homeward direction and away from Stan. Now or never, the arrows seemed to say, their flashing a bleating of envy, an aching inside. Each time she seemed to miss the right moment to slip through the changing lights, her truck hurtling through amber lights turning red. It seemed to happen over and over.

A few blocks from home she heard what sounded like a wailing baby. Distant, and then growing louder, following right behind her. The swirling lights chasing her were red and blue.

She needed this like a hole in the head. Flubbered her lips in a big sigh, like a horse blowing against the dust. Pulled over and rolled down her window. She wasn't in the mood for questions.

Something in the young cop's face reminded her of Stan. A tendency to squint with one eye, to wait before speaking, then talk in a calm, I've-got-you-covered voice.

"Did you know you ran a few lights back there?" he asked, his flashlight searching inside the truck.

"I couldn't seem to get the timing right," Leigh said, laughing to hear how stupid that sounded. At least it was honest.

The cop had dimples where a slow-spreading smile might be starting up.

"Have you been drinking tonight, ma'am?"

"Nope. I spent the evening with a newborn: we were all of us—my ex and his girlfriend—having tall glasses of juice. Well, and milk for the new mother." It felt clean to be telling the truth. Like a fresh start to something.

"Would you mind stepping out of the truck? Giving me a little walk down the road?"

Leigh unfolded her bare legs beneath her short skirt and hopped down. She was so tired she felt droopy and none too steady on her feet.

The cop was shaking his head, holding out one of those dealies to read the alcohol roaming around in your blood.

"Would you mind?" he asked, holding the doodad to her mouth.

She had a sudden urge to laugh aloud. Blown kisses, she thought. Bye, bye baby. Give Mommy and Daddy a kiss. Send a few to the gods watching over you.

She puffed out her cheeks, but couldn't get the damn thing to work.

The cop was smiling widely now, the dimples taking over his face. He had a cleft chin too, she discovered while standing next to him.

"Let's give it another try, shall we?"

"I couldn't get those plastic whistles you got in cereal boxes when I was a kid to toot either," she said, as an excuse.

This time the reading was good. And proved her to be right on the money. She hadn't had a sip of a drink all night.

The cop looked surprised. "Just a bad driver then, I guess."

She felt a bit miffed at that because she was damn good when it came to hauling the sorry asses of those horses fresh off the track. Had to give them a smooth ride or they'd go haywire. But she decided to play it meek and mild, not sassy, said, "I guess I didn't have my mind on the road. Was feeling sad about a few things."

He knew it was about love, she had as much as admitted it. Plus he could probably read it in her face. How she was sorry to have hurt Stan and to have ruined it for herself. Sorry to have acted so stupid.

She got back into the truck. He seemed to be writing her a ticket, but when she looked down, she saw it was only a warning. To proceed with due caution through intersections. From a Constable Harry Leggatt.

"If you're ever sad again I may have to call you on it," he said, trying to firm up his voice. But he still had a grin tucked away in those dimpled cheeks, she could just tell.

"I hope you do," Leigh said, smiling back at him, relieved to be off the hook. "I'd smarten up in a real hurry if you told me something twice."

She watched in her rear-view mirror as the cop trudged back to his cruiser. He had a bit of a stoop to him, she thought, like Stan did after years of bending over his guitar.

The police cruiser turned around and drove away. She drove carefully the last few blocks, just in case. Sat in the truck before the darkened house she and Stan had lived in while making up their minds about country music.

That Harry cop was sure cute. She knew he would stay in her mind like a second chance. Or a third or fourth or fifth chance, she couldn't remember the odds. It was one hell of a long shot, but still.

LIKE A BRIDE

In our small town, International Women's Day was marked by absence. Any honouring of women happened almost by accident, a few arcane exhibits on a token table during our spring festival on the Easter long weekend, and thereby a full month beyond the designated day in March, as afterthought. As if we couldn't figure out what to do with women, whether as resilient housewives or renegades who might have asked for better pay running the old telephone office at a time when there were still party lines with everyone listening in. Which sounds like it was way back during the war but it might as well have been yesterday; nothing much had changed since women went to bed using Coke cans as hair rollers.

My mother had a picture of a few women with placards, wearing those wide pants over boots which was all the rage during the eighties, protesting something nuclear, maybe Chernobyl. I was in a stroller at the very edge of the shot, a small blur. My mother said she'd been disappointed more people hadn't tooted their car horns as a show of support. Instead, people had looked at them as if they were madwomen.

It was plain that women still lurked in the background at our spring fair, mostly as volunteers, with pie contests (the women baked them, the men gobbled them) and a quiz tent, which was like speed dating with local history. You had to pull cards from a deck, held by some brat who'd always wanted to be smarter than his teacher, and answer the questions: Where was a fossilized dinosaur bone found nearby? (And by a woman of all things.) When did the one-way bridge over the river give way to flooding? (Most women didn't drive yet, so it wasn't a woman who got washed over the edge, though a certain Mrs. Barnstead helped rescue a man who'd been swept away.) The card with a photo of bathing-capped women in woollen swimsuits—they looked like women wrestlers without the spandex or the muscles—posed the question, Where was the old swimming hole? (Beneath what is now the library.) Along with the trivia, there was always a children's talent show on the main stage, all girls because it looked too gay, as my clueless brother said, for a boy to sing or sashay in wannabe-Elvis getup. So that left bossy little girls with batons twirling, small bums waggling in their spangled suits; it looked like a sexual dance with kids scarcely older than toddlers. In other words, borderline creepy.

"That's very American," was my mother's take on the way the mothers fawned over the poor knock-kneed kids with their high, whiny voices as if there might be Hollywood agents among the few dozen bystanders. She usually took part in a few events: one year she laid out an exhibit of posters and magazines on a series of old ironing boards, one wooden one so lopsided it looked homemade by someone not great with tools. My father described it as my mother "pressing home a point" while he pretended to touch an old steam iron that hissed and spewed, and grimaced, said "Ouch!" My mother said there was a certain "irony" to him having said that, and only cracked a half smile.

"Your mother was always a rabble-rouser," my father said of her exhibit. He had to stop himself from saying *shit disturber*, which amused my brother no end.

"You see what we're dealing with," my mother said, nodding to me as if I were recruited to her team, my father and brother on the other side.

My mother's display featured an ad from the *Women's Weekly* magazine from way back in the sixties with a woman preening while doing housework just to please her husband. He, a clean-cut cowboy in a wide-brimmed hat, standing just beyond her kitchen window with a wide-eyed horse. So soon enough he'd be tracking in the mud and the hay from doing a man's work and she'd be tickled pink to start up the cleaning all over again. There were even older ads for floor polishers and vacuums that supposedly freed women, but I found the fact that women bought these devices from shady-looking men in suits at the front door somewhat depressing. As if they had nothing better to do, neither the women nor the men.

When I was seventeen I looked at it this way: if a boy—or even a full-grown man—wanted to look stupid as can be in a baseball cap, whether backwards or forwards or tipped up from his head like a two-year-old, nobody stopped him. He might never have played baseball at all and didn't need to keep the sun out of his eyes when he was sitting at the dinner table. It was just an excuse to never comb his hair or to look as if the world revolved around him when it didn't. As if he might be boyishly forgivable no matter what. Whereas if a girl—let's just say me, for example—wore a hat like that, she was told she was a tomboy, or it didn't suit her, or the way she was wearing it was all wrong, the haranguing went on and on.

That's pretty much what I thought in 1998 about International Women's Day.

My dad called the springtime frolic Creek Daze, as though Tramner's Creek with its six thousand souls (the population kept dwindling) were in a trance ushered in by the fortune teller's tent, off in a discreet corner of the baseball diamond so people could go there without being seen. My sister had gone to scout out her future the same year she got pregnant and then lost the baby: God knows what the woman with the scary deep-set eyes and muumuu foretold. She had a business card, Beatrice the Sayer, and read tea leaves and palms and talked in a ghastly nether voice straight out of a graveyard. She swore she could broach unresolved grudges with dead relatives and read the mind of your dog or cat too if you brought her a picture. I wouldn't have dared subject our dog, Bailey, to her hexes; as it was, he howled like a lunatic on full-moon nights.

Our hokey spring fairs were intended to lift spirits after the long winters. There was no reason to think that one in a year nearing the tail end of a century famous for its terrible wars and gobsmacking technology, with all its vaccines and insulin and penicillin and antidepressants lending us longer lives, would be any different. Not until Marcie Wanderlust—that was her real name, except you pronounced it the German way, with a sharp *V* sound, pressing your upper teeth into your bottom lip and growling in your throat—had that moment in the dunk tank that looked like a splashy striptease.

It wasn't usually a woman who took the plunge, and certainly no teenage girl wanted to be gawked at like in some freaky wet T-shirt contest. It was usually somebody's dad, someone important, like a high school teacher or bank manager, even the mayor, so we could all laugh at someone we were intended to admire. The men often wearing those woollen long johns from way back when because the weather was often still cool and breezy. The tradition may have started with the fact that our little crossroads of a town was named after a pioneer who fell into the creek during the freshet. People variously claimed he'd been a fur trader and others thought farrier, but one thing was for certain, he'd been a Tramner, his family roots coming from a place named Bridlington in Britain, famous for its beaches and lobster fishermen, and, during the war, its spies.

The dunk tank had been newly updated from the big old plastic tub that looked like a horse water trough: now it reared up like a giant aquarium filled with blue chlorinated water above the bystanders, who no longer ran the risk of getting splashed, which had been half the fun. And here stood Marcie, in a wraparound sheath dress with a long slit up the side and a gaping neckline; she hovered on the platform for ages, smoothing her dress down and inflating her ample chest by holding her breath. Her nostrils seemed to be quivering, her eyes fixed on some point in the distance. The mostly young boys in the lineup to get people wet—it was some sort of charity event for kids with terrible diseases—were too stunned to actually throw the ball. They didn't want to ruin the view, but prolong it. Marcie's grim-faced husband, Heinz (we all called him Ketchup behind his stiff back) finally threw the shot that plunked her into the water, whereupon the dress ballooned up to her waist with a lot of bubbles, her legs thrashing about, a dark swatch of something that looked like pubic hair straying from her twisted panties, her breasts bobbing to the surface first, like a life vest with nipples. Her big brassy hairdo flattened against her skull and gone to ruin. She was laughing—hysterically, it seemed to me, but still laughing. It was hard to say whether she was happy or not. Shocked was more like it.

Heinz was in charge of the town's water system; he kept the tap water from tasting bad in late summer, and saved local wells from getting toxic from all the runoff from local farms. So at first people thought it to be a stunt gone awry. That he might have put her up to it as a symbol of water conservation or something. Or maybe she was supposed to say something and forgot her speech. But the look on Ketchup's face didn't seem to be onside; he was clearly outraged, and led Marcie away by the wrist—roughly, it seemed to me.

"That was a gong show," my brother said, as though at fourteen he'd seen a million half-naked middle-aged women. I couldn't imagine my brother having a girlfriend any time soon, although he was going to need some help keeping his mouth shut.

"Yeah, poor Heinz the Water Wizard, he sure won the booby prize," my father added, while my mother made a face like one on a cat grimace scale that tells you when your pet pussycat, who doesn't have the right words in English, is feeling pain. Apparently the ears are drawn back, the mouth is pursed, and the whiskers lie flat against the face.

"What I meant," my father continued, "is that she hurt his pride."

"Hurt *his* pride?" my mother responded, clearly exasperated.

Right then I knew my mom and dad were going to have one of their silent fights. Which could go on for days, a creaking sound of eggshells as we tiptoed about trying not to make things worse.

Why Marcie had done it became the stuff of rumours. Was it impulse or premeditated? Her being all dolled up seemed to indicate the latter—but why? Was Heinz fooling around and this was comeuppance, or was the straitlaced Heinz actually gay? Was some trouble at home the reason Marcie had run for school trustee as an attention-getting device the year before with her tottery platform shoes and her big bouffant hairdo? A scarce few had voted for her. Nobody thought of Marcie as provocative or particularly brave or bright, but then nobody knew her very well; Heinz always seemed to speak for both of them.

Reckless or not, I knew why she'd done it. But I had no words for it—and feared being disbelieved or dismissed had I shared what I knew to be true with my quibbling parents. That would have been more unbearable than the thing itself.

I would have talked to Amy, but she'd recently gotten herself to Toronto as an aspiring actress. She'd been cast in her first feature film, a horror flick, because she'd acted terrified in just the right way, blood packs squirting like mad in the pivotal scenes. I think the two-bit director was hitting on her, but what do I know? I've never yet been smitten, as my father would say.

Apparently I'm too smart for my own good, as my mother—my old mother, before she got carried away with her new-found feminism—used to say, meaning I had to protect some pathetic boy's ego and go with the flow.

"I don't blame you, boys at your age act so stupid," she says now.

"How old were you and dad when you started dating, or whatever?" I naively thought to ask one day, hoping to lighten the tension in the house.

"Old enough to know better," my dad said, reverting to his old comical shtick before stopping himself. It was the stopping that had me worried. They were still fighting, I guess.

"We were young by today's standards, perhaps, but not then," my mother said tartly, and that was all. She made their romantic heyday sound like one of those sweaty interviews where you hope to hell you don't get the job, and then you land it. As if at first you're afraid of not being good enough, and then you're too good. There was none of this schmaltzy *Oh, when I first saw your father, that's when I knew* bumph.

The clocks had sprung forward but something in our house had gone back to the steel-edged days of winter. There was a frostiness in the air, a taking of sides on every subject or remark, my brother and father on a team, like a scoffing pair of disaffected teenagers. I wanted to side with my mother, but was frightened of her sudden new vehemence after her years of patience and seemingly not caring about my father's missteps.

It was as though Marcie's bravado had infected my mother, and she, Edie, would do something less foolhardy and more telling. She took it upon herself to expand the hoopla on behalf of women the following spring. Her booth—it had gone from a few rickety ironing boards to a booth—would feature videos and interviews with women soldiers, scientists, storytellers, the first Canadian female astronaut and the shark lady from California, who swam with those freakish fish for years and found them to be, for the most part, gentle creatures. My mother had found a police officers' manual in a used bookstore which she said "explained everything." The small maroon book held that a police officer's job was to "keep the peace," that a man's home was his castle, and described women to be largely unreliable as witnesses, even to their own mishaps of family violence or attacks from strangers, due to their Marcie-like attributes as sexual beings, luring men toward "carnal knowledge" and thereby toward understandable jealousy and rage. Women were just chattel, after all, and had to be kept in check. They were just as untrustworthy by dint of their flighty minds as their culpable bodies, as evidenced by their superstitions, how they just *knew*. Women like our own Beatrice, who offered spooky premonitions in the fortune-telling tent, being liable to be arrested. In this handbook women were lumped in with witless children and so-called idiots—as people with disabilities or special needs were called back then, much to my mother's horror—they were all foolish beings needing protection. Even from themselves.

My mother showed me this book in a huffy mood, said, "Not that long before you were born, imagine!" She seemed to want something from me in response and I didn't understand what. I could see that it was inscribed to a certain Constable McQuaid on a front page, wishing him good luck in the year 1949.

"That was ages before I was born," I spluttered, "twenty years before the man on the moon!"

"Well, it takes much longer than that for the human heart to change its mind," she said then, which didn't make a lot of sense. I was confused with all the talk about castles and chattel and carnal knowledge, of hearts and minds being tangled up, and how old I was in relation to life being a joke, as if it were somehow my fault.

My father could feel the ominous shift in the family weather, knew that his years of telling tasteless jokes about the Irishman, the Englishman and the Scots undertaker were numbered. Or that one he always repeated, with slight variations: What's the difference between Zsa Zsa Gabor and Brigitte Bardot? The answer having to do with wearing furs and wearing nothing—I could never remember the gist of it.

If this deep-freeze in our house kept up, there would be fewer men at the next spring shindig, I could just tell. Not if their wives or girlfriends made them visit a booth where they might learn something new and disturbing about women. I mean, who needed reminding about rapes in Rwanda or clitoridectomies? I couldn't even tweeze a stray hair near my bikini line without my eyes tearing up.

"Let people take umbrage if they feel so inclined," my mother warned.

If she had her way, the dunk tank would go missing, along with the gaggle of little girls swinging batons and wiggling their hips. And bye-bye Beatrice. Instead we would draw a new crowd with a farmers' market of organic foods all grown by women, and female folk singers from as far away as Nelson, where a lot of draft dodgers had put down roots, or even from Washington State where they'd come from in the first place with their gutsy songs of protest. It would be our own homespun Lilith Fair, she said. I thought she meant Lollapalooza, so I said with some enthusiasm, "Great, Mom!"

She was clearly on a roll, promised a walk-through exhibit like a hall of mirrors: one hundred inspiring women in one hundred years of Tramner's Creek, heroines we'd never yet heard of. One who could predict the wheat yield on the Prairies down to the last bushel, and another who was the fastest typist west of the Rockies. My mother had had to dig for her heroines in a town of only ten thousand, even in the long-gone boom years, had even gone back to Bridlington to find some of her candidates. I found some of the suffragists' faces scary, I have to admit. As though they would have gladly died, or killed someone—which apparently they did, with a bomb in jolly old England—just to give me the vote. The mood had changed, as though Marcie was the opening act to feminism decades too late in the formerly dazed Creek. I could sense a certain uneasy nostalgia for flawed families, everyone clinging to worn rituals and old roles while my mother surged on. We were raw, newly exposed, open to ruin.

That was when it began. My waiting for or willing something to happen—dark, piercing, unforgettable. It was not love I wanted—not if it ended in what my father and mother had bowed to, and were lately somewhat fiercely resisting. I did not want things to stay the same, all prickly with meaning, but I didn't want them to get worse either. I was upset with Marcie and didn't want to pay the price of her floundering courage, as my mother saw it, or cruel betrayal, as my father seemed to feel. I was unable to side with either one of them, was still a child dreaming my way down the highway on one of our old Sunday drives, bound to be dissatisfied. There was wandering in me, disillusionment. I wanted to be "knocked up" in the way my father had described Amy getting pregnant—as in *woken up*. Altered. Taking nothing and no one for granted.

I was about to graduate from high school and maybe leave this dinky town and my tensed-up family forever, yet I had no idea of what or who I wanted to become. I just didn't want to make any haunting decisions I might regret later. I had to distance myself from my old amiable mother, her willingness to please and adapt, and stay away from the new one as well, with all the sharp edges.

I asked her one day what her favourite colour was. She looked surprised, said she didn't know. "I've never really considered it," was what she actually said. "Does it really matter?"

"Yes, it matters," I shouted, throwing down the laundry I'd been folding into a heap on the sofa. She was hopeless. How could a woman go through life folding turquoise towels and not see a dunk tank with someone thrashing among waves of aqua like a drowning woman? How could she not burst into shrill fits of laughter, Marcie style, when pressing the stiff cuffs and collars of my father's "good shirts," worn on occasions he described as "behaving himself." As though there had to be a restraint put on a man's tendencies to overreact, to seem too strong or too weak, and often they looked to be the same thing, a man acting the fool. I was angry and afraid; there were all these links crackling in my head between clingy dresses riding up women's thighs in dunk tanks and my father once seeming innocent and now seeming to mock my mother, like two sides of a coin in one of his old tricks, heads or tails, win or lose. The spinning coin of my childhood had lost its shine.

It didn't help that Marcie got breast cancer and started wearing outlandish clothes and wigs in defiance. All the fashions of the sub-Sahara or the Punjab, of the Maori or complete with the vivid face painting of the mother clans in outback Australia; she was the world in all its loose folds and bright colours, and the world had become Marcie. But a wig of blonde dread-knots, really? Marcie as a Rastafarian?

"We shouldn't pity her," my mother said. "She's found herself."

But I couldn't see how. Except for the fact that Heinz had left Marcie—or maybe she'd left him, I hadn't considered that possibility. In any case he'd taken a new job in a town with a bigger water tower, so perhaps she felt relief on that score. That she could die of cancer now and not simply of shame.

I'd had an inkling weeks before that last infamous spring fair that things might fall apart at our house. There was still a scatter of snow on the ground, patches of bitter brightness against the incoming dark of late afternoon. I'd been taking the shortcut home from the library, where I'd been trying to finish an essay, when I had seen Marcie in the car. They had been parked behind the school, at the end of a road only the workers used to cut back trees at the edges of the playing field. And I was walking with my shoulders raised against a raw wind, my hood drawn down. So at first I thought I'd imagined the way Marcie was hiding her face in the passenger seat, trying to ward off his blows. He was striking her, again and again, and it looked as though she might be bowed down forever from the weight of his attack.

I felt bile rise in my throat and wanted to run away. But I didn't move, I just kept willing things to stop. For an instant Marcie straightened up somewhat, raised her head, and then she saw me. It was as if her eyes were asking me something, and I had no answer. And then Heinz saw me too, and flashed me a terrible smile, more of a snarl really, his teeth bared. That was when Marcie left the car, and walked straight toward me, as if for safety. She wasn't running, but walking slowly, in measured steps, like a queen or a bride. While Heinz did an about-turn with the car and fishtailed away.

We simply passed each other, never saying a word or really meeting one another's eyes a second time, Marcie heading off into the woods behind me. I stupidly imagined her going to a cubicle in the library—there were only three—and burying her stricken face in a book or perhaps hiding in the washroom until closing time. All I knew is that she was walking in the opposite direction to her home. And all I kept hearing, over and over, was a series of dumb expressions people used on a daily basis: *if it comes to blows, when push comes to shove, they had a real dust-up,* or *it might end in fisticuffs,* all the sayings we spouted as if they were hollow, empty of meaning. I wondered if it was only a matter of time before my father might strike my mother, my mother cowering. I wondered at all the things done behind closed doors in Tramner's Creek that might need a reckoning.

* * * * *

As it turns out, International Women's Day is not so international; it's an official holiday in only twenty countries, women given the day off work so they can spend more time with the children and do more housework, while in a dozen more, men bring women flowers—big fat hairy deal. It's still the whole being-put-on-a-pedestal notion, and never mind equal pay or having say over even their own bodies. A whole lot of places do nothing to honour women, not the Czech Republic or even the United States, who have long held suspicions of anything vaguely socialist in nature. And in some countries, like Pakistan, it's just plain dangerous to even raise the subject of thanking women. You can get killed for such an idea. No matter what the UN says about improving women's lives, the world's a mess, and there's still war and poverty, too. So it wasn't just our lacklustre little town that let the ball drop. Into the dunk tank, as it were.

My mother's efforts on behalf of women pretty much flopped the following spring, and put the entire notion of the spring fair in jeopardy. A wicked thunderstorm came up out of nowhere—totally out of whack for that time of year—just as a few singers were about to take the stage, and the sound system shorted out. Everyone disbanded and took shelter in their cars, got the hell out of there. Seconds later and someone could have been hurt; it left a bitter taste in everyone's mouths that wasn't just from the blown-down tent with the smokies and sauerkraut. We could all feel the charge in the air, how the tone of our spring festivities had grown to something more serious and broken in spirit, disjointed. It seemed people had wanted a dunk tank and a fortune teller and a tacky talent show, even though they might have said later that it was all too old-fashioned and that's why the whole shindig folded. I felt bad for my mother, who paid the singers out of her own pocket because the audience had skedaddled and there were no donations; it was the right thing to do. I felt even worse when my father went back to telling his old jokes—*well, at least she got thunderous applause*—and they fell flat too. We were all afraid of having to change, that much was clear.

That was five years ago, and the town I grew up in has now changed to suburbs, all spread out, where people no longer know each other's names. Sometimes things happen so fast. Like the way Ted and I had our first fight the other day. Although we have not made plans—we've only slept side by side the whole night a couple of times—we have already embarked on a life together, as my mother would say. The two of us buying groceries the other day felt so in sync, and thereby so precious, I could hardly breathe. Sometimes we can see through each other right to the end of things. We feel an equal measure of surprise and comfort, try to keep a balance. Try to remain somewhat of a secret to each other, like a gift you keep giving slowly, just to prolong the anticipation of joy on another face besides your own.

So it was totally stupid, our argument, a misunderstanding where one had assumed something and the other had mistaken good intentions for bad ones. That's all it takes sometimes, I guess. Or maybe we had reached a point where we were testing it a little: you have so much love and then you want even more.

One or the other wanting to be hurt, and then saved, pulled back from the edge. All I know is that when Ted raised his voice, I suddenly saw Marcie again, although I had tried for the longest time to push the scene away.

"Don't hit me," I said, when I had not expected to even think such a thing.

Ted looked so anguished, I thought I might never retrieve him from the dark. A shadow fell over him, fell over the two of us. And although you can punch a hole in a shadow, it's still there.

"Why would I ever want to do that?" he asked, in a creaky voice, choking back tears. He embraced me then, so carefully and softly, as though I might otherwise break to pieces.

He was the first person I ever told about Marcie covering her head with her arms and turning away from her husband's blows, and even then I couldn't find the right words to describe the look on her face when she first saw me.

ONION

We fought about it, surprised to find what was at stake.

Practised quibblers, we knew enough to trade a few threats and barbs, then work out a rough truce. This is mine, you can keep what's yours. No crossing the lines. He was typically the first to let something go, I would stubbornly hang on, pursue the argument to its vanishing point. There was a back-and-forth about it, a kept balance. After carrying on about some you-forgot-my-birthday thing, we would simply carry on.

He mentioned going to one of the peeler bars downtown with a few pals from work. As if he'd had little choice but to tag along with a herd of thirsty men drawn to an oasis. The drinking hole being the Bird of Paradise, an older joint in Vancouver, been around since the sixties. When we all burned our bras and became accidental feminists, screwing any long-haired guy in sight, free love and lots of it. So I knew the strip club was there, like you know pigs are kept enclosed in steel stanchions in humongous barns, are hellishly butchered, and you still eat bacon. I know there's hypocrisy and denial, and we all take part. I know that, I said to him, in a voice I wanted him to hear as assured and not hysterical.

Dave said, "Don't get all worked up," as he tended to do. He was simply lazier than I was emotionally. That didn't make him my guru.

He told me about the strip joint almost too casually, daring me to make a fuss. Which may sound strange, but that's what people do, put a few things at risk. Just to stir things up, see who's minding the store.

"No big deal," he said. "Not worth keeping a secret," but I still sniffed deceit.

I'm a linguistics nerd, like to dabble in undertones, what's *not* said. Like to know how things begin, why they persist. And I'm good at it.

My specialty is the language of sexual connotation. I've been under a lot of stress lately, everyone on edge these days, looking for any shocker reason to bring down a promising actor or politician, my once semantic niche now considered the everyday weapon of whistle-blowers. I was recently roped into being a so-called expert witness to determine the "toxic environment" of a workplace. I was asked to consider what so-and-so might have meant when he said, "Look at you, you're beautiful! You can have anything you want." I had been told to dress sensibly, look trustworthy, not too much makeup or too little flashy clothing. Which was interesting in itself.

"I'm stuck between a rock and a hard place," I said to my attentive jurists, knowing the phrase to be a lame pickup line. "I mean there are so many shades of grey," I continued, dredging up a bestselling novel of creepy seduction that was read—let's get that clear—mostly by women. "It's a slippery slope between good intentions and offence taken, and a woman being rubbed the wrong way—please excuse the pun—either learns to care less about perceived intrusion or insult, or else goes looking for recompense. I wouldn't say money always eases the pain; wronged women often just want a heartfelt apology."

The prosecutor in the case against a seedy professor type was chewing the inside of his cheek in consternation, and the defence team was holding back smiles. I was proving to be a perfect example of how words can grow murky in meaning. For clarity's sake I threw in a few illustrations. "It's complicated," I said, "like putting a keepsake away in a safe place and not finding it later, because our safe places keep changing. People say dumb things, that's a given. My mother once said to me, 'Don't dress like a tart or you'll be treated like one.' I was going on a date with a long-time friend I later married. But I knew she loved me and meant well. In fact I think she wanted me to dress *more* like a tart, make a bigger effort. Protest can often be camouflage."

There was an eerie silence after I stepped down from the stand. Where I had sworn on a bible to tell the whole truth. I don't think the courts will be calling on me again any time soon. What I'd wanted to say was that we're all confused, both men and women, and the truth lies somewhere between being innocent as a newborn and totally irredeemable; it's hidden to us until it's too late. None of us is really clear on what's happening *while* it's happening. All I know is that love often requires a sacrifice. It's an ages-old theme, as old as the storied bible used to hold us to account.

Dave had disappointed me, that was the point. *Above* and *beyond* seemed appropriate sentiments for what I'd hoped. Were there any retro frat parties scheduled, I sneered, or any wife slaps recounted among his buddies, any she-deserved-it stories, hardy har har? Clearly I *was* getting worked up, which only made me angrier.

He looked shocked, unnerved by my venting. As if he suddenly recognized me to be a woman, a stubborn creature somehow linked to those scantily clad girls on stage, and was puzzled by that. Was I fighting *for* them or *against* them? In any case, I was more finagling and less fun than he'd imagined.

"Listen," he said, trying to take my elbow before I veered away. After ten years of being in cahoots, I actually felt a certain distaste. The world as I knew it, floating like a bright balloon escaped from a birthday party and bound to pop sooner or later, with Dave and I watching to see when that might happen, had gone flat. I suddenly doubted our entire marriage, that we could still go the distance.

"It's tame stuff," he insisted. "We go there for the food—"

He stopped when I rolled my eyes like a grade eight girl, and snapped, "Liar, liar, pants on fire, nose as long as a telephone wire! So this is a favourite hangout!"

He squeezed up his face as if listening to a strange sound in the house. As if we were being quietly robbed. "I've been there a couple of times, sure." Then he added, "These girls are treated well, if that's what you're worried about, they prance in the background of our banter about boring tax writeoffs and where we stand with our testy clients. So what's the big deal, we're grownups, aren't we? Above and beyond this sort of spat."

It haunted me that he was acting so predictably. And that I might be too. He'd used my own unspoken words to turn the tables: *above* and *beyond*. So maybe I was old hat, and he knew me better than I thought. But what did I expect? He was a tax lawyer, his motto, "exemption, not evasion." His work was finding loopholes, and with his dark curly hair, boyish air of golly gosh in his midforties, he nicely lowered the bar on being forgivable.

"Okay," I said, taking the bait and running with it, "I'm a big girl"—I pushed up my not-half-bad breasts in his direction—"I'll come along for lunch, try out the good eats and take in the scene of beer-bellied, guilt-ridden losers who *don't get any*, as they like to gripe, as though their sex drives are over the moon and they need teenaged twins to satisfy the itch. I worked in places like that, waitressing, don't forget—I know all about guys who protest too much while leering at girls with fake hooters."

He could see where I was heading, and he didn't like it. Our quick and desultory love life of late, his paunch, my puckered thighs. Things were picking up pace.

He kept making it worse. Told me then in our sun-bright, once-comforting kitchen, what a realtor had recently told him. That his toughest sale was that of a biker house in the suburbs, two steel poles installed in the pricey, updated kitchen. When the prospective buyer, a woman, had asked about these oddities, thinking structural problems or some design fad, the realtor had to keep a straight face when he said, "Exotic dancers."

"In the kitchen?" She'd been stunned by the thought of fat-slob motorcycle gangsters working up an appetite.

"Needless to say the would-be buyer wasn't amused. Or maybe she was. 'Cause he still closed the deal. So you never know," Dave reported. "I mean, if I'd been that woman, I'd have worried about a murder in the house, never mind a few girls dancing for tips."

If this was Dave's idea of "life is strange," I wanted to make it even stranger.

"Well, you're *not* a woman, as it turns out," I said. "Let me know what day we're doing lunch at the Paradise," I shouted, slamming the door behind me. "We have a date."

* * * * *

What to wear, I wondered, looking at my generous outline in the mirror. I am what's described as a husky girl, which can mean strong and sporty, the sort to play along with the boys in a whipped-up bout of hockey on the back pond. She might even be good enough at stick handling to beat them at their own game. My voice has always been tomboy hoarse too, like a blues singer who smokes and drinks too much. A real turn-on for some guys, including Dave. Or at least it used to be.

It occurred to me that we hadn't gone out together for ages; my body looked like it was pouting. New pouches and dimples of flesh at my armpits, belly button. Most nights we grabbed a quick bite in front of the TV, then fell asleep, not exactly in each other's arms. We were in dangerous territory, I knew that. Hadn't exactly been learning anything new and enticing about each other.

I could be a good sport, doll myself up a bit, don spiky heels, some midday cleavage and a frazzled, right-out-of-bed hairdo. Men of a certain ilk liked that. And I have a good head of hair, I've been told. Streaks of gold amid the darker bits of ash blonde, and lots of it. Dave would be nicely surprised, taken off guard, if I pouffed up my tousled look, donned some lipstick. But who was I kidding? I was on a reconnaissance mission and this was war.

I'd told my friend, Suzette, of our little spat. She's French and fearless, said, "Go in drag!"

"What? As a guy?"

"Yez, this is what I'm thinking. A three-piece suit, smoking a cigar, as a charade." Which she said the French way, to rhyme with facade. "And every now and then you clutch yourself, like a baseball player, to remind everyone of your HOOGE package."

She was stick thin and beautiful, could probably glue on a goatee and pull off a gag like that, have the guys at her feet. So

I deferred to her advice in my own scattershot way. Pulled on a pair of old scuffed cowboy boots, baggy-bummed jeans and a loose sweatshirt Dave had given me—it was one size too roomy, as if he thought I might soon grow into it—the logo on it reading *Compromise Sucks*. It had been another of our feuds; I didn't like him slouching around in his sweats, and he'd fired back with the hoodie so I could look equally sloppy around the house. We'd laughed at the time, but I had to wonder now what he'd wanted to say. Never mind, it was a perfect look for the occasion at hand. No man with a roving eye would find me appealing in this getup. I'd be as invisible as the proverbial fly on the wall. Maybe Dave could just say I was his long-estranged sister or something.

I arrived late, just to let Dave imagine I might be a no-show. That I'd caved.

But no sirree, I entered the dim lighting and the dank smell of spilled beer like I was part of the mafia clan that owned the place. With the Cuban heels on my cowboy kickers, I stood slightly taller than Dave: he had to reach up to give me a peck on the cheek, a startled half embrace.

"She's doing research," he said, when the threesome of men looked abashed. "Undercover," he said, with a hint of scorn in his voice. "Let me present my wife, Anya. With the beautiful high cheekbones," he added, to remind the boys I might have better days as a looker. "She has a doctorate in picking apart language. What every word means when we spout drivel. So watch your mouths."

Clearly not his trophy wife, was the answering buzz in the air. One fellow, named Stanton—a silver-spoon-in-his-mouth, born-to-be-a-law-partner type—raised his eyebrows and said, "So this is—*Onion*?" before Dave shot him a dark look.

I could see that Dave had spilled the beans. A delicate part of our private history. So much for intimacy, I thought.

When we'd first met, Dave had forgotten my name almost as soon as he'd heard it. He'd recalled only a vague vowel sound, an echo of my introduction. To cover his mistake he'd acted the fool, had asked, "Your name is Onion?"

"Yeah," I'd sent back at him, "it's Swedish for tangy and sharp, can make even a strong man cry."

Right from the first we'd been all taunt and pushback, like kids thrown together in a schoolyard, reluctant friends too unnerved to admit affection. He still called me Onion sometimes as clumsy endearment. It was a reminder that we hadn't fallen hard, as some people describe love, but slowly, one thin-skinned onion peel at a time.

A lot of things were coming to light. Dave's promised girls "in the background" were right in our faces. We were sitting under the sequined crotches of two women strutting about on the bar-as-stage in a choreography weaving from one duct-taped X to another. Under the garish pink and blue flashing lights they looked older than I'd imagined, closer to thirty than eighteen. And in their strange getups, leather bustiers and metal-studded belts like comic book superheroes, seemed even more tawdry. Younger girls might at least have been working their way through student loans and having a good laugh.

I'd had a pal in university who'd written romances for some pyramid scheme called Matinee Desire; she didn't get rich quick but it paid some bills. She learned the "pink ink" formula like a pro, a woman swept off her feet by some swashbuckler's approach across the dance floor—his eyes burning like dark coals, her halted breath in her taffeta dress as he held her tightly—we'd mimicked all the lines. My friend had plucked some of her scenes of women succumbing—you could only hint at the tryst, never describe anything too salacious—from her mother's accounts of dating in more constrained times. She'd given herself names like Amy DeGauche or Lexie L'Amour and her mom, an avid church-goer, would have been shocked to learn she'd unknowingly read some of her daughter's drivel. Which only goes to show we all have double standards. Say one thing and do another.

The real-life girls sashaying above me were winding up their spiel, the electronic music veering toward humpa-bumpa and impending crescendo. The twosome took off their skimpy tops and twirled them, their breasts hanging like grocery bags injected with silicone. Not pretty, I thought. And all this time I'd worked out at the gym, just to keep my puppies up and somewhat pert.

There was a reluctant round of clapping and wolf-whistling, out of duty, it seemed, more than enthusiasm. I felt a sadness come over me, a heaviness in the room. Everything slowed to a crawl, somehow out of sync, the girls retreating down their little walkway to a backroom for a toke or something stronger—the one named Taffy with an audible sniff-sniff—and who could blame them? I myself needed to down a second sidecar with its warm whoosh of brandy to keep my spirits up. I tried to imagine my sex-kitten names as a take-it-off dancer. Maybe Tallulah, with a wide drawl from Texas, wearing nothing but a red bandana and a pair of chaps, my ample ass sticking out from the leather leggings. Or maybe I'd appear as the one and only Onion, a kind of stand-up comic peeling off layer after layer, fur jackets, rain slickers, flannel full-body sleepers—the sort that kids wear—flinging my clothes every which way. It was the sort of thing that Dave and I might have laughed at once. When we were still a couple, *above and beyond*.

I felt unmoored, at a great distance from Dave. Who hadn't said anything to me, had his head together with his chums, seemingly preoccupied with business spiels. I had been betrayed, made the butt of a long-standing joke. I had a knot of what seemed like major heartburn in my chest—but was only a building rage.

"I asked you to hold the onions," I said loudly when they brought my greasy burger, but Dave pretended not to notice. Just as I'd suspected, the food was no great shakes, too salty and chewy, had simply been a lame excuse to watch bump and grind.

I took only a couple of bites, had peevishly lost my appetite.

Onion? Seriously? My old flame, Dave, the love of my life, had a few things coming to him. What else had he shared with his buddies? I felt antsy, ready to change the mood in the dump. Dave was being an asshole, had no right to give me the cold shoulder, treat me like the original bad date. As not good enough. He was clearly making his point and I felt compelled to make mine.

High time for me to make a few new friends on the fly. As the one and only Onion—freshly peeled. Tart enough and just enough of a tart to make a strong man cry. I jumped up from my stool and vaulted handily onto the stage. Nothing like being sporty if you're wearing the right gear.

I started with the Charleston, some flapper moves from way back in rum-running times, my hands switching back and forth over my knees, had myself some fun as a warm up. One of the girls looked back through the parted black curtains, her face creased with worry. "This is not about you," I said. "You girls were great." As if I'd been made captain of their team and they could trust me to figure out a strategy, still win a losing game.

Without music to shore me up—there was only baffled chatter from the tables watching me—I had to hum a little ditty while swinging myself playground-style round the baby-oiled pole. *Ring around the rosies, pocket full of posies, husha, husha, we all fall down!* And almost right on cue, down went my baggy jeans: one snap and a quick zip, though the cowboy boots slowed things down. I had to kick them off, the way you do when you're sixteen and your boyfriend is shrilly waiting to get into your knickers. Then peel off the knee socks I'd worn so the boots wouldn't chafe, the way they always did. I felt a cool breeze rise between my thighs: I was wearing a pair of Dave's boxers with a fetching pattern of fleurs-de-lys, for that risqué French touch of *je ne sais quoi*.

"Whoa, bring it on sister!" someone yelled from the shadows. There were loud hee-haws, as if a street person right off her nut had just crawled out of a dumpster half-dressed and they might as well enjoy it before the cops were called.

I was feeling the anger now, seething, as I bumped my tush against the steel pole and ran my hands up and down the shiny surface. I could see my image in the metal, all wobbly and bent out of shape, like a sumo wrestler in Dave's shorts. But there was no time to hesitate, feel sorry for myself. I had to find a groove, some on-and-on percussion line to carry me, and fell into a medley of old-time rock and roll, a little bit of Creedence "rollin' on the river," added a few croaking refrains from Rod Stewart and did my best Mick Jagger strut, ranting, "You can't always get what you wa-ant," then threw in a few salty licks from J. Geils, "It serves you right to suffer, baby," while spreading my thighs behind the pole, rising and falling, rising and falling. Let me tell you, that move is really hard on the knees.

I didn't dare look at Dave, although I thought I saw a smeared reflection of his face, red and distorted, in the mirror behind the bar.

There were more jeers then, and some lout groaning, as if in fake pleasure—or real pain. The bartender was wide-eyed and not yet willing to stop the show. He was a balding man with hefty shoulders, like a built-in bouncer, and I thought he might have a smile hidden beneath his growly mouth. I could almost feel him cheering me on.

I stuck out my fanny and waggled it a little, golden retriever style; if they wanted a piece of tail, they could have it. A small crowd was milling closer to the bar, as if at the fringes of an accident, just to see the damage. And feel themselves spared.

"Oh baby, oh baby, shake your booty," I whisper-shouted; in the heat of the moment I couldn't remember whose ass was up for grabs, or what it was, exactly, that I wanted. I was stoking hot in all the commotion, so pulled my hoodie over my head, my frazzled *Last Waltz* T-shirt riding up too, giving the crowd a brief peekaboo at my jouncing tits in my killer black underwire bra. It was like a wet T-shirt contest without the wet, and for one freaky moment without even the shirt, before I righted things.

"Stop!" someone shouted in a high-pitched voice I took to be Dave's. "For God's sake, just stop it," he repeated, reaching out for me from the bar stool below.

"Ah-ah-ah, no touching the girls—you know the rules," I said, making a shocked face at my milling fans.

"Yeah, buster, leave her alone," someone shouted. "She's having a gay old time up there!"

"Probably *is* a lesbo," entered the fray, "but who cares?"

I was trying to dream up a finale, wanted to end on a high note, maybe with that Freddie Mercury scream, the bit at the end of "Bohemian Rhapsody" that sounds psycho. I wobbled a bit on a pirouette, had to give it to the girls for staying up on their toes in their heels. My legs were actually cramping. Nerves, I thought, and remembered to breathe. Tried to imagine all the guys in the room butt-naked. Which didn't really help.

There wasn't a woman in the mix, as far as I could see, not until the female cop came in, all bustle and buxom in her uniform, and motioned to me to get on down from my gangplank. I had mutinied from a ship of fools and there would be hell to pay. But wait a minute—I wasn't the one who had betrayed our marriage. It was Dave, my husband of old. My late husband, Dave, my dead-to-me dear heart.

So this is Onion? I still couldn't believe it.

The officer was waving me down; she was short and squat, weighed down by her black clunker boots, wasn't going to make it onstage to grab me. So I took my own sweet time to wrap things up. Said in my sulkiest, burnt-out rocker-mama voice, "I just want to say, you guys are sure old-fashioned, have good manners. Thanks for listening, 'cause I'm a newbie at this whoop-de-do. My version of old-time burlesque. And I want to thank my hubby, who loaned me the clothes for this occasion, want to say, thanks honey. Thanks for the memories."

And then I slipped deftly off the stage—fell, more like it—into the waiting arms of that burly officer who smelled oddly of black licorice. I'd had a friend in grade school, Astrid, she was Dutch, who'd sucked on the stuff all the time, would show me her black tongue. I couldn't remember now whether sarsaparilla was a close cousin of anise and whether that counted for anything. I just wanted to find something that was true and undeniable, wanted to hang on to it.

The cop escorted me gently to a back door with the sign, *Fire Exit Only*. We stood in the back lane for a bit just shooting the breeze, me shivering in Dave's gotchies and my bare feet, she gallantly placing her cop jacket around my shoulders.

No one else saw us, and Dave didn't come to collect me.

"I haven't been drinking," I said to Constable Dvorak, her name reminding me of cellos scraping out a sad music. "Just a couple of cocktails, nothing serious, and I'm not a druggie or certifiable nutbar. I was just pissed off with my husband—and I feel better now, I really do."

She ran through a few charges she could lay—disorderly conduct, public mischief—while taking down my particulars, that I was working on a grant at the university, lived in an upscale neighbourhood. Didn't have a shrink and wasn't depressed.

"No medications?" she asked. She actually looked concerned, which I appreciated. I suddenly felt like bawling my eyes out.

I could feel my nose going red the way it did when I tried to hold back tears. Dave had often enough pointed it out: that was usually the sign for him to give me a hug even if he didn't have a clue what was going on.

"Never been much of an escape artist," I snuffled, "more the facing-things-head-on type. Played goalie in college soccer, almost went pro."

She was squinting at me, trying to detect some loose screw she'd missed.

"Well then, you're free to go, I suppose," she said. "I may give you a call later."

I looked down at my skimpy attire and held my hands out in plea stance—no pants, no keys, no car. I'd come on the bus so I could drink oodles and not drive. But that wasn't all of it. I'd been hoping, against all odds, that Dave and I might still come out on top. That we might have a chuckle at the bar, toss back a few and feel somewhat reckless, might grab a taxi and go home together, jump into bed for an afternoon nap. Something we hadn't done in ages.

"You've got no one who can come and get you?"

And I suddenly recognized the exact moment, the point of no return. When Dave had reached out to me in his stung pride. Still trying to save me from myself.

"I've got no one," I said.

"I'll give you a ride home," she offered.

* * * * *

And that was that. Dave didn't come back, not that night and not for weeks. I thought maybe he had disappeared without a trace, the way people do when there are no right words to say goodbye. That maybe he lived in the Caymans now, as a tax dodge.

He finally sent me an email that read, *You showed me up to be what I am, only human. Good for you. And you were right, those girls aren't living the life of Riley. We'll split things up fairly.*

There was clearly no fight left in him. I had to wonder whether he had said all he meant to say, and who Riley was. Made a mental note to look up the expression.

Months later I saw Dave cross the street in a hurry when he saw me. I thought I recognized the girl he was with, wearing a faux-fur coat even though it was spring, a radiant sunshine angled between the high-rise shadows. It was only when they were out of sight I realized she was one of the dancers at the Paradise. Big tits and tawny hair, tottering along beside him in her over-the-knee boots as if he were her knight in shining armour. Not too garishly young for him, and maybe just pleased enough with his sudden empathy to be free of the skin trade.

I was walking the rescue dog I'd brought home for company. The pit bull–doodle didn't really like any tension in the air, so I didn't bother to shout or wave at Dave. At first the dog had whined and scratched at his confines, left his initials on every door, and he still needed constant reassuring. But I could tell when I scolded him for walking on the dining room table—as if on a peeler bar, wary of strangers and being touched—and he grinned at me, baring his teeth in shame, that he was finally getting a sense of humour.

TWINE

She had crossed the border from Canada when it was still dark. When asked her reasons for travel, she had blithely said, "Tying the knot—you know, getting married."

The stiff-necked guard hadn't cracked a smile. And usually people did, even offering congratulations, as if declared love were some sort of lucky field goal.

"Well, not today," she'd added. "Today I'm just buying the dress."

To which he'd replied, "You'll have to pay duty on the way back, ma'am."

The ma'am had bothered her, as though married might soon mean old hat, over the hill, wearied and worn. So she'd thrown a salacious grin his way, had said, "Oh, don't you worry, it'll be worth it."

She'd found the dress by chance, an hour across the line, in Bellingham. In a tiny shop called Vivienne's, cramped with half-dressed mannequins. Had tried it on in a hurry, twirling once before a mirror and leaving a deposit. She'd promised to return for a proper fitting. It was a vintage design of ivory satin, one of a kind, chaste looking with just a dash of off-the-wall skittishness. She liked it for its slightly madcap quality: the off-kilter sash, the believe-it-or-not bustle, the teeny, V-shaped dropped waist, so Shakespearean. "It looks like you're embarking on an adventure," the dressmaker had said, squinting through her wire-rimmed John Lennon–era glasses, her face framed by long, straight folk-singer hair. "It suits you."

The dressmaker, who wasn't called Vivienne, but Hilary, had said to arrive shortly before the shop opened. Before the hordes of young brides, she had said, with a distant Brit accent beneath a wider American twang. Clare couldn't imagine this hole in the wall to be a favourite among brides, but had been told theatre people came here for outfits and alterations. Hilary had exuded the opposite of high pressure, more a thinking out loud, on the fly. "When you come back," she'd said, "don't wear a lot of makeup. I think you'd suit a fresh-faced, might-have-eloped look. And you could wear sandals if you wanted, Greek would be nice, and I'd lift the hem a little—but wait a minute, how tall is your beau? Well then maybe you don't want to seem too diminutive, want to be holding your own next to him, what do you think? Yes, so maybe bring along a pair of heels."

Clare had liked Hilary's take on things. Such a relief after the women with powdery complexions and raised faux eyebrows at the chi-chi shops in Vancouver suggesting her hips were too thin for this pouffy style, her collarbone too sharp for that scooped neckline. They sized you up as you walked in the door and started herding you, coaxing and clucking, these women all girdled and cinched into place, insisting on lace sleeves or florets on Clare's slim backside that would waggle a little as she walked down the aisle. The operative word—*flattering*—as though you were a flawed bride from the get-go, needed shoring up for what they named the biggest day of your life. As if the rest of it—her desire, and not just for her soon-to-be husband, but for a whole world of possibilities, for children (or maybe not), for a roomy house with veranda and flowering trees beyond (or something else entirely, perhaps years of travel, of ambition or compassion, working for a non-profit in the sub-Sahara or teaching hard-bitten kids in Belfast or Bangalore), she had so much choice she could scarcely breathe—would end in disappointment or regret unless reined in by a proper dress and making the right entrance as a bride.

Now she had arrived in a part of town with century-old brick storefronts, low-rung carpet and furniture stores, ceramic tile distributors, and bay windows hung with Tiffany lamps, as if someone might still want one of those clunky eyesores. She lowered a window, peered at addresses as they sifted by in the grey-flannelled fog, the streets near the harbour drifting off at unexpected angles due to the shifting shoreline. She could hear grinding machinery from a nearby factory and cars swishing by occasionally in the wet streets, but the early morning had an uninhabited feel. All the sounds of traffic somehow suspended, as if vehicles might be slightly off the ground or still some distance away around corners you couldn't see.

She remembered the shop to be next to a manufacturer of brass fittings and three doors down from a bakery sending up sweet plumes of steam. She had almost passed it when she spied a small window with the name *Vivienne's* in gold lacy typeface, a green-tarnished copper awning over a door of cracked black paint. She pulled over quickly to grab the nearest parking spot—in a metered zone, but she'd only be a minute. A nip here, a tuck there. She shivered and wondered whether she was too early, took a brief look in the rear-view mirror. Her face looked somewhat out of focus in the semi-dark, a few faint lights glimmering here and there through the shrouds of fog spilling along the shore.

She pushed the car door open and swung her long legs into the cool damp vault of air; the feeling of heels and stockings beneath a short dress was one of being too naked, too tall. She unfolded into the street, her skirt clinging with static to her legs. As she leaned back toward the car, to hear the small click of the power locks, the air seemed to move in a giant wave, pressing her legs flat against the wet fender of the Honda, bending her upper body sharply over the glass of the small car's windshield. She heard what seemed to be a high-pitched scraping, of something caught and then released, then her own sighing, as though all the wind had gone out of the world.

* * * * *

The tall young man climbing toward the street from his below-ground flat was running late: he still had to walk a few blocks. He took the stairs two at a time and liked the way his head and shoulders arrived at street level before his legs found the sidewalk. *Head and shoulders above the rest*, his father used to say of his expectations regarding his lanky son. It had given the youth a stoop early on.

On a clear day he could see the ocean down the hillside, hear the conniving cries of seagulls as they wheeled through the air. But today he couldn't see more than a few paces ahead, the fog was so thick. The sounds of the unfolding city seemed distant, unreal. Closer at hand he could see the strand of garden twine hanging from the railing at his stairwell. He'd first seen it from his front window a couple of days ago, waggling in a breeze; it made him think someone was there. He'd meant to cut it off; it was tightly knotted and too tricky to untie. It bothered him and yet he hadn't bothered to remove it. That had to be some sort of character flaw, he thought wryly.

He wondered who'd put it there. One of the actors always scooting into the place next door? It was some sort of artsy-fartsy costume shop with zany mannequins in the window, soldiers or pirates, sometimes flappers from the twenties. The place was really popular at Halloween. Or maybe the string had come from one of the near-homeless kids that kicked about here. They squatted in the empty old factories below him by the harbour, where they did their skateboarding stunts over handrails or along the crumbling sea wall. Maybe it was some sort of message, like an inukshuk. *I was here.* Well, two could play this game, he thought. He'd quickly add a sheepshank knot to the end, one he'd learned in his summer-camp days, and shorten the twine's sway, see what happened.

He was stooping to twist the twine when he caught sight of a body flying through the shrouded air. The figure hovered for an instant over a small hunchbacked car, and then plummeted. It was too early in the day for one of the daredevil skateboarders. He could tell it was a woman's shape, slight and slim; she whimpered a little upon landing, the sidewalk too slick for her to regain her feet. She seemed to be having trouble even sitting up, was holding the left side of her face. Fell once more to the ground, her head making a dull thud against the pavement.

A stout figure in a raincoat was running away into the swirling mist, screaming hysterically, "Did you see that? He just drove away. Jesus, he just drove away!"

That was when the young fellow realized the flown form had been struck by a car. He hadn't seen the vehicle, only heard a high-pitched engine whine receding into the grey-veiled morning's light. The upset woman was click-clacking up the sidewalk, still shouting to anyone who might be nearby, "Stop that car! Stop that son of a bitch!" her outrage at the runaway driver overriding any immediate concern for the victim collapsed more or less at his front door.

He stooped to check her face; her eyes were dark and wild like those of a bunged-up animal on the side of the road, looking for escape. Her hands were opening and closing, her throat making a sticky choking noise. He tipped her head back slightly and the sound grew softer, her breathing easier. She was well-dressed, with a short, old-fashioned bouclé jacket—his mother had worn such a thing—over a dress, the skirt torn along one thigh. Probably one hell of a bruise, and he hoped nothing was broken. He lifted her then, against all warnings from his high school lifeguard days—people could break their necks off a diving board—and carried her down the half dozen stairs, leaning against the wall while he unlocked his door, pushed his way sideways through the hall and deposited her carefully on his sagging sofa. She murmured something that sounded like thank you and he thought she couldn't be that badly hurt if she was so polite.

He stood by his small front window and watched the commotion outside; the shrieking lady had come back with a companion—a man in a business suit. He could hear the woman's exasperated voice. "But where did she go? She was right here. I mean, she collided with a car—has to be hurt. Where did she go?"

The distraught woman was showing the man in a clumsy charade how the victim had rolled, even bounced, over the front of the car. Had fallen just there. She picked up something in the gutter then, what looked like a spilled handbag, and seemed to be holding a shoe as well, a single high-heeled shoe. That seemed to finally convince the fellow in the suit, who pulled a cellphone from his pocket and started walking into the fog, talking. Looking to the left and right for some woman who'd perhaps dragged herself to a nearby doorway.

The young fellow might have gone out the door right at that moment and motioned to the pair, might have said, "She's right here. The woman hit by the car. She's here." But he hesitated, distracted by the fact that the injured girl—she was younger than he was, he thought—was trying to say something. She was obviously winded, needed a moment to get herself sorted out. Some colour had returned to her face—in fact a huge purple bruise was starting to creep in, beneath one eye and over one cheekbone, all of which thankfully looked to be in the right place. She had fair hair swept to the side of her pale brow—those long bangs that made girls tilt their heads in listening—and a delicate face. And she could speak, although only in whispers it seemed. She asked him what time it was; he would remember that. And when he said, nine o'clock, almost right on the nose, she added, "Thanks so much, Brem. I slipped a little in the street, you know. But I'll be all right. Don't worry, the wedding's still on." And then she started crying, in small, chirping breaths, like a flow of childish hiccups.

He bent over her, pulling his old mohair blanket to her chin, propping up the pillows behind her shoulders. Felt the pulse in her wrist, which was solid and steady, given the circumstances. She didn't seem to be in shock, only somewhat confused. And he said he didn't mind being a little late for work, that it was no trouble at all. And when he looked back to the window, the couple outside had disappeared from view.

Well, they'd called for help. He could just keep an eye on the girl in the meantime. Soon enough there'd be a cavalcade of first responders and second-rate cops combing the area; he didn't have much use for cops, carried a bit of a grudge.

She slept then, lightly and fitfully, waking every few minutes and looking startled. He didn't know if he should allow her to drift off, given the risk of concussion or coma. At one point, when she woke up and smiled at him, this incredible warm smile that could have heated his crummy old apartment for an entire dreary wet season, he asked her to move her fingers and toes so he could measure the danger she might be in. She murmured something about him being so silly, then wiggled long, pale fingers, all ten of them, one with a discreet diamond on it, as though she were in fact intending something serious with someone. Then he pulled up the blanket from her feet, which were curled childishly around one another, perhaps for warmth, or to cling to some lost sensation of gravity. She obediently waggled her stockinged feet and he rubbed them briskly, like he supposed a doctor might, and said, "Well, that's good. That's just fine." And she smiled her look that said, you have always been so foolish, and closed her eyes once more.

He drew down the venetian blinds to shut out the rising light and the hissing of tires on the wet streets. Then tiptoed into the adjacent bedroom, so as not to disturb her, and phoned in sick to work, said he had stiff muscles everywhere, probably a flu. Not a good idea to come to the office and spread it around. It was Friday and people checked out early anyway if nothing big was cooking. They had started this thing of wearing blue jeans on Fridays and heading home or to the bar not long after two o'clock, business permitting, without a stitch of guilt or any thought to make it up on Mondays. Profit schmofit, Mack said, and he was the boss. He was also an alcoholic who made things up to suit his needs. So he made some joke about Kevin having had a little too much to drink, no doubt, and yeah, he should sleep it off. He'd be right as rain and ready for Saturday night if he took care of himself, was all Mack said.

It was easier to give Mack some lame-assed excuse than feed him any incomplete story about the girl. Mack would only razz him and make up some spiel about how the girl had gotten there. Something sleazy, no doubt, wink, wink. He'd be no help at all in setting things right, Kevin figured.

Saturdays they went out carousing, as Mack called it. He was always trying to set Kevin up with some flirty girl not his type while Mack continued burning all his bridges, as he'd done first with his ex, and then with the girlfriend who'd caused all the trouble. What *was* Kevin's type? He'd never figured that one out; surely no one like his mother, who was sharp-tongued in commandeering his father—there was persistent underlying blame in her voice—and not like his sister, Ella, whom he hadn't seen in ages. She'd been flighty in mood but funny as hell in the things she dreamt up or said. She was younger in age by a couple of years, but she'd been the ringleader, always the one to push her more reticent brother across some line. And they'd gotten into trouble, with the graffiti they'd sprayed on the stalled trains by the port, anti–Gulf War stuff. And once they'd tied tin cans to the principal's car, as a reminder that the old codger was married while fooling around with a too-young student at the high school.

He and Ella had been close—thick as thieves, as his father used to say with some good humour, and never said anymore—until she'd inexplicably disappeared. She had never once since that day ten years before made contact with Kevin. He knew she was a survivor, probably still earned a certain notoriety, maybe now as a surfer or bartender in Belize or Bangkok, or maybe teaching English in a posh school for expats in some country broken by constant civil war. That would be totally up her alley. He could understand her not giving away her whereabouts to his parents; they'd had a lot of conflict. Had an especially big row the night before she'd skedaddled. But not getting in touch with him had left Kevin bereft and baffled. As if she didn't trust him to keep a secret.

Kevin felt the girls who sometimes cozied up to him at the bar were like Ella, bound to betray his loyalties and affection if they seemed rambunctious and carefree on the surface, as she had. When these girls asked him questions of a personal nature he always clammed up. He seemed older than his years with that crouch in his stature, and a somewhat receding hairline, his less than brash manner. He was twenty-eight, full of regrets regarding his own apartness and kept them largely to himself. He had come to believe that holding back gave you a little more clout.

He was lucky to have his job, he knew that. A techie geek with a start-up that made gadgets called Slo-Pokes, walking sticks to help the elderly or those with disabilities get about. They were like bendy ski poles with flexible bits to absorb shock, adjustable for anyone with a crooked gait—quite the improvement on crutches or canes. And they were selling like hotcakes. If this girl had any trouble walking after this stunt, he had just the thing to help her get on her feet again. He wanted to share this with someone, how odd life was sometimes, so random and yet seemingly connected. He could have shared his predicament with Ella if she were here—she would have known what to do next. He could almost hear the taunt in her voice—"So, what, you scooped a girl off the street and now she has a headache? I love it. That's so you, Kev."

It had always been so easy for Ella to go against the odds and come out smelling like roses. She'd had a good sense of just how far to go: when she'd been called into that principal's office for the tin-cans deal and he'd asked her in his smarmy manner why she'd done such a thing, she'd answered, "Because you're a friggin' pervert. Everyone knows you're bonking a student—that's disgusting!" You had to love a girl who could say that to someone's face. It got her suspended for a few weeks, but the principal moved on by year's end because the vice-p, a woman, had been listening in.

If the day had started quickly, in a measure of quick footsteps and hectic shouts, it slowed and expanded to a sense of time having stopped altogether. The girl slept for several hours, his three rooms, set below the random rat-tat-tat of passing feet and the swishing of cars, otherwise silent. He lived beneath the small shop of a locksmith, an older fellow who came and went as he pleased. Today there were no sounds of grinding keys or of hammering at a spent lock. There was a surprising intimacy, he decided, in watching a stranger sleep, the rise and fall of the blanket with her quiet breathing, her small sighs and frowns, as if she might be dreaming. He sat and watched her the entire time—or that's how it seemed, although he might have dozed off for a bit in his old tufted armchair.

* * * * *

It was well after noon before the fog lifted, a smeary sunlight filtering through the closed slats of his blinds. When the girl had finally stirred, he could see she'd been cold in his dank little suite, her knees drawn up, the blanket having slipped to the floor. So he'd given her a robe to wear over her torn dress, one his mother had given him and he'd stubbornly never worn. It was maroon, a thick plush terrycloth, and swamped her. She looked like a small forlorn child in its folds.

He said to her, "A little big, I know, but that colour suits you."

She seemed brighter, was sipping gingerly at a cup of tea.

Was she hungry? he asked. She shook her head in reply. And winced, as though the slight movement had caused a fleeting pain.

He himself was feeling light-headed, he got like that if he didn't eat. He'd looked in his fridge and there was nothing much there, not even eggs or milk. He ate mostly on the run, grabbed something from the takeout joints in the market by the harbour. You could pick up almost anything, from local oyster burgers to Asian stir-fries. On weekends he brought home small bags of fruit or meat, freshly baked bread to tide him over.

There was a sudden loud knocking at the door. The girl's eyes opened wide, and something like fear seemed to flicker through them.

"Probably just canvassers," he said. "You know, election time. They'll go and bother someone else soon enough."

He went to his window and peered obliquely through the slats of the blind. Whoever it was had already vamoosed. He heard voices next door at the neighbour's costume shop, Hippy-Dippy Hilary's. He could vaguely make out a slim someone with a pulled-down fedora and what looked like an Army & Navy greatcoat, the kind they used to wear in the sixties. So not a political go-getter, after all, but one of those kooky actor types at the wrong door. But he felt jumpy and put out, as if the girl's presence were to blame for his not having groceries, for his lack of civility in answering the door.

"Don't you have to be somewhere?" she asked then, as if the knocking had reminded her of some previous way of living.

"Uh-uh," he said. He had to stop himself from saying, not until tomorrow. And Mack was sure to come looking for him if he didn't show at the local watering hole. He felt a hot chase of apprehension in his gut—he'd crossed a threshold by stepping into the thick of things, every gesture now freighted with new meaning, startling consequence.

The girl looked like she was welling up, close to tears. She put down the tea, her hand shaking. Worry edged across her face once more.

"Why is everything silver, like light glancing off tinfoil?" she asked.

He didn't understand what she meant. The room was dimly lit, and he couldn't see anything that might be shimmering. He followed her distracted glances toward the stove handle, then to a small vase of deadened flowers. A girl at the flower stall in the market had pushed them into his hands a few weeks back. "Take them home to your honeybunch," she'd said. "They're fading fast." He hadn't realized until later that she was giving him an invitation to say, "No honeybunch." To start something up.

The girl on the sofa was staring at him with a puzzled look, as if the sight of him were unsettling.

"I can't remember what you look like," she finally said. She held the flat of her palm to her left temple.

"Hey, listen," he said. "Do you want me to get a cool face cloth or something?" He poked his head into the freezer; not even a bag of frozen peas. He should have thought of ice hours ago. For her face or her leg; her entire body was probably aching.

But she said nothing in reply, her eyes darting about the room again, trying to focus, find one familiar thing that might jog a likeness, a memory.

He might have consoled her then, said where things stood, that she'd had an accident. And he might have picked up the phone, even then, and made a couple of calls. It should have been simple, the next sensible thing to do. But something stopped him, an eerie sensation of being out of sync, dislocated in time. Of hovering, unable to act. Like one of those dreams you have of showing up for an exam on the wrong day, the room empty. And you're still trying to find your pen.

He offered to make her some chicken soup, though he had none of the fixings. And he couldn't leave her alone, run out to the closest corner store; she was too helpless. In the freezer he had a chunk of leftover duck, already cooked, that he'd brought home from his mother's some time ago. It would have to do. Comfort food, he thought. That's what she needed. He plunked the poultry, hard as a rock, into a pot, threw in some ancient bay leaves and a bit of savory. Put it on to boil. Maybe he had a wizened carrot somewhere, or some canned corn or beans to give it some heft.

He was feeling increasingly raw and unnerved, impatient for the next thing to happen. Like an actor waiting in the wings for some right cue to enter the scene. This wasn't turning out as he'd expected; his impromptu guest wasn't exactly bouncing back. She was looking more and more on edge and exhausted, in the way those two sensations often occurred together. She had dark circles under both eyes, not just the walloped one.

It annoyed him that the cops hadn't showed yet. They were probably checking the hospitals, seeing whether the runaway driver might have stolen the car or had since showed up at a body shop. He knew all about that from first-hand experience way back when. They were all paper-pushers, those guys. Stuck in their rote protocols and routines, and they'd only give him a hard time for dragging her in here off the street.

"We'll have to see about getting you home," he said brightly, "now that you're feeling better." He felt like a cake sparkler about to fizzle out, an awkward celebration just about over.

"But I *am* home," she said with a frown. "You're always teasing, Brem. As though I'm a child, needing constant amusement," she added, forcing a piqued smile.

This is when it starts, he thought. The blaming. All it took was a few hours and a man could be accused of almost anything.

The few shambling relationships he'd had with girlfriends of any sort had all ended badly. There was always something he'd missed seeing entirely. The women miles ahead of him, leaving when he was just beginning. One of them had said, "You don't have a clue, do you?" And no, he hadn't had any inkling as to whether she was happy or unhappy. He'd been totally baffled. But he didn't let it worry him; as far as he was concerned, women were all pretty crazy, his mother and Ella among them. You couldn't please them, that was the thing.

He wanted to correct this sad-faced girl, remind her that he wasn't this Brem fellow. He realized then he didn't even know her name. Much less where she belonged. Thought peevishly that the pair who'd grabbed her purse and single flown shoe knew more than he did, and how unfair that was. The girl was clearly bonkers, delusional. Had seriously hit her head.

The soup was boiling over, and he turned it down, a heavy steam filling the air. Again there was a loud banging at the door, a thumping. Insistent, like the heavy sound of someone demanding entrance, fists held sideways.

"There's somebody home—I can smell food cooking," a raspy male voice said from the stairwell. The racket at the door continued.

"Be right there!" Kevin shouted. This was what he'd been waiting for, he thought, a sensation of here and now, of push coming to shove.

He guided the girl unsteadily from the couch to the bathroom; she was dragging a leg now, as if one side of her body had grown stiffer, unwieldy. He lifted a finger to his lips while he softly shut the door. "We don't want you getting into trouble," he whispered, winking. As if they both now shared a pivotal secret.

The knocking grew harsher. "Police. We want to talk to you. Open up!"

He cracked open the door, fiddling with the chain, and saw two hefty officers, one just a kid, really, with smooth, unperturbed features, and the other more grizzled, with grey at his temples and an unshaven look to his heavy jowls.

"We're looking for a missing person," the older one said gruffly, pushing his way through the narrow doorway once Kevin had freed the lock. "She was hit by a car this morning—we have a witness."

He realized he hadn't thought of what he would say, how he would let the story unspool and be believed. He wanted to buy himself some time in the telling.

"Well, I heard some shouting on the street, just as I was leaving for work," Kevin offered. He had the impression of watching himself from a distance and was pleased with his response. He thought it struck just the right tone—concerned and somewhat confused.

"Can you give us your name?" the older cop asked.

"Kevin McFedden," he said quickly, although for some reason his own name sounded false, made up. Like a foolish jingle or rhyme.

"So, Mr. McFedden, did you see anything out of the usual when you went to work?" Baby Face asked. He was like a giant toddler, an oversized head and stubborn paunch on widespread short legs. Chubby fingers resting on his holster, as though it were a toy gun and he was playing his part.

"Just thick fog, and that's not really out of the usual," Kevin said with a tight grin. But he could see they didn't want to talk about the weather.

"And when did you get back? From work, I mean," the older officer asked. His eyes were scanning the room, the blanket on the couch, the scarcely touched cup of tea.

Kevin looked at his wristwatch. He realized with a shock it was after three, the light dimming beyond his shuttered window. The fog creeping in again.

"Well, I came home early—wasn't feeling well," he said. He thought that might explain the tea and the blanket on the couch. "Was just cooking myself some chicken soup—it's actually duck." He wondered why that detail might matter, what sort of poultry. But he wanted to seem on the right side of honest.

"Anyone else in the household see anything?" Baby Face asked. His hand was still at his hip, at the ready, as it were. He seemed to be listening to something. Kevin realized it was the sound of running water down the darkened hall.

I live alone, Kevin had wanted to say.

A strained singsong that sounded like half sobbing, half laughing was coming from the bathroom. There was a despairing cry then from the girl: "Oh no! How can I go anywhere looking like this?"

He'd forgotten she hadn't yet seen her battered face.

"Hey Mr. McFedden, who's that?"

"A friend—she needed a place to hang out for a bit. You know, bad boyfriend sort of deal." He was amazed how easily candid-sounding answers came to mind, as if he had a sudden knack for spinning lies. But it seemed he had no choice; he could hear how everything that had once been the truth, only this morning, would now ring false.

"Yeah, well we'll have to talk to your friend."

The girl obediently emerged from the washroom, as if she'd been listening, but she was edging along the wall as though she might otherwise collapse. She'd taken off the dressing gown.

The older cop was shaking his head grimly, looking at her bruised face and torn skirt. "Can you give us your name, miss?"

"Maybe—Clarissa?" the girl began, as if someone might correct her. "No, that doesn't sound right—sorry."

She was careful not to look in Kevin's direction, he saw that.

"Can you tell us how this injury happened?" The older officer was touching his own face to show her what he meant.

"I found—a dress, the sort for a bride." She flushed, then paled again.

"Do you remember where you live?" the officer asked gently.

"Here?" she asked, with a quaver in her voice. She plainly looked bewildered and once again close to tears.

"Before here," he asked again. "Name of a town—or a country?" He was trying to coax some right response from her, say anything that might ring a bell. "No idea? It's okay if you don't recall—you've had a scare and a bad fall. We'll find out."

She was sinking to the floor, sliding down the wall, her knees buckling. "The man in the dark," she murmured, "didn't smile."

The head honcho was calling for an ambulance, loud static filling the room as voices crackled back and forth. "Yep, think we found her."

Baby Face was crouching beside the girl, easing her from her crumpled seated position to the floor. "I think you need to put your head down, miss. Are you feeling dizzy?" Her head sank to the floor, her fair hair spread across the purple shag carpet. It bothered Kevin to think he hadn't vacuumed in a while and that she was lying there, her knees shuddering, as though she might be frightened or in pain. "We're getting help," Baby Face was telling her. "You're going to be fine."

The older cop took a tour of the premises, stomping to the bedroom and back, then stared hard at Kevin. He was gnawing at the inside of his cheek, taking his time to keep from getting too riled up. "You've got some explaining to do, buddy. And don't jerk me around. I need you to get it straight."

"I found her on the street," Kevin began, "but I didn't see what happened."

Why did he keep brushing aside the real story, he wondered, when he hadn't done anything wrong? It was as if he were being trapped by the way they were treating him. "I wanted to give her some time—to collect herself, sort herself out. So I gave her some tea, wanted to make her some soup." That was true enough, but he could hear how bad it sounded to be doubling back on the soup excuse. First for himself, then for her sake. He regretted having taken the damn bird out of the freezer, how the broth smelled greasy and none too appetizing.

"Listen, I don't care if it was tea or if it was fucking duck soup. What I am interested in is why it never occurred to you to call for help. She's clearly injured. People would be worried, looking for her. So do you have something to hide? Do you usually do things all on your own? What—you some kind of superhero or something?"

"No cape," Baby Face said, smirking.

Oh, they were a real comedy act. You saw it all the time in hokey action flicks, Kevin thought. Two cops on the beat, wisecracking all the way to a grisly crime scene. He'd always found it so clichéd and phony but it seemed to be true.

"Yep, we got a live one here," the older officer said. "Well, we're bringing you in for questioning, Superman. Maybe you're the one who hit her, bumpety-bump, then tucked her away for safe keeping—what do you say to that, Mr. McFedden?"

Kevin felt a surge of panic that he could be accused of such a thing. "I don't ha-ha-have a car," he said. "Don't even der-der-drive."

He hadn't stuttered since he was a teen. It happened for a while after his sister had disappeared. And he wanted to mention that: how the cops at that time had done fuck all, had said his parents had reported her missing either too late or too early, he couldn't remember the spiel—they'd said she was just a runaway. Just. That they couldn't put every kid's face on a milk carton; she was of legal age and would show up sooner or later. His mother was mobilized by rage, hanging posters of Ella everywhere, which he'd then ripped down, thinking they would only make Ella stay away. His father silent, as if Ella wasn't worth all the fuss, and Kevin stammering all the time, unable to trust his own voice. He'd been a nervous wreck, had barely finished high school—and that's why he didn't drive. Like a total idiot he'd hit a lamppost after failing his driver's test, had smucked up his father's car without even having a licence, and his father had *lost faith in him*, that's what he'd said. And he wanted these knuckleheads to know that. But he couldn't get out the words; it was like going back to some previous beginning and end that went on and on, where he was always the last one to see a thing clearly. Always the fool.

"Yep, yep, yep, cooking duck soup, a real homebody, when you should have been call-call-calling an ambulance. Dialling up the local cop shop. Oh, you're in the soup all right."

Kevin could hear the cop mocking him. He wanted to paste him one right in the chops. He wasn't a total weakling, worked out sometimes at the gym. He wanted to have one of those struggles where they twist your arm behind you and hold you to the ground. It's supposed to hurt like a bastard. Sometimes they dislocate your shoulder or break something. You always feel sorry for the bad guy then.

Still, he was glad they were taking the girl off his hands. There had been a brief instant, right at the start, when he might have become someone else. One of those grinning guys who protested later at being called a hero, said, ah heck, I just did what anyone else would do. They usually downplayed having run into a burning building or saving someone from drowning. Some sort of brave, knee-jerk response. But he had been tested in a small, delicate moment, like a tricking of memory—that's all it had taken to make him lose his bearings. He'd been helpless to do the right thing, he could see that now.

Strangely, he felt relieved. Until this morning he'd always pushed away the thought that something bad had happened to Ella. Had made it her fault. She was headstrong, took all sorts of crazy risks, thought only of herself. But he knew now it wasn't her fault.

He felt a pressure long held inside him ease a little. Well, just wait until Mack and the boys hear about this escapade, he thought. And the girls always hanging about in the bar: here was something to hold their interest. He'd doctor it up a bit, make it sound as though he'd called the cops right off the bat and it took these jerks ages to arrive. But he'd be laughing in his self-deprecating way, describing the girl swamped in his dressing gown calling him by her fiancé's name; he might even mention his stab at making frozen duck soup.

The medics arrived then—it hadn't taken them long—easing a stretcher down the tight stairwell and into the room, lifting the girl just so—one-two-three, hup, keeping her neck supported— they had it all down pat. And she said thank you. Just as she had to him.

He didn't know how to say goodbye to the girl who wasn't named Clarissa. Good luck? Hope you find your dress and it fits? Hope to hell your marriage works out because so many don't? Hope your head doesn't hurt too much and you don't have a blood clot the size of Texas behind that pretty face? He felt sorry for her, really bad about her bunged-up head, but he also felt a cold pity for himself. How he'd foolishly gotten caught up in this whole ordeal. So he gave her a wan smile and simply shrugged his shoulders. But she turned her head away.

He felt listless, bone-tired, as if he might actually be coming down with something. As if there might be some truth to what he'd said; he couldn't keep it all straight.

He turned off the broth then, shoved the steaming pot into the fridge. He'd have to skim off the fat later; his mother had shown him how to do that, with cheesecloth. Or maybe he'd just toss the whole works out.

"What a crock," the older cop muttered to his pal.

"Of duck soup," Baby Face agreed, as if he'd seen it all, when he didn't look old enough to be in a bad-ass garage band.

Kevin had nothing else to say. His stammer would only trip him up and they'd share another laugh. He was sick to death of these jokers. What the hell, he'd kept the girl safe 'til the twosome arrived in a frenzy at his front door. There was nothing criminal about that, and there hadn't been any force on his part, or hanky-panky. Wasn't that what these guys always worried about? Some low-life conning a sweet young thing and helping himself to sexual favours? He had simply tried to keep things from falling apart—the way things did some days, like when your sister asks you to bring a shitload of money to a place in the middle of the night and you don't even find the note from her 'til it's too late, then can't find the bloody money she's stowed under the bed in a paper bag tied up with garden twine with a zillion knots so it can't be easily opened, and the whole time you're trying to be dead quiet so you won't get caught by your feeble parents, your hands shaking, and when you finally hit the streets and find the warehouse down by the harbour, it's long after she's expected you and she's gone. Without a trace. And you leave the packet anyway in the hope that she'll return for the money—and God knows where she got it—and she no doubt loses the whole stash to some crackhead who picks it up, no questions asked. And for years afterward you're just trying to piece it together, all the jagged bits, but you can't keep the right picture in place. Of where everything belongs.

And today it hadn't taken him sixty seconds, right at the beginning—when he'd lifted the girl from the ground, and she'd seemed so light—to seriously fuck it up. He guessed it was all a matter of right timing and how confident you felt about your own chances. He should have left her in a heap on the sidewalk, that's what he should have done. Trusted those other two busy-bodies to take over. Lesson learned.

The two officers walked in tandem, the older one in front, Baby Face puffing up the narrow stairwell behind Kevin. As if he might make a run for it or something. As if he was dangerous, right off the wall, one of those mental cases they sometimes had to round up. Baby Face with his pudgy hand on his holster, as if the young stooge would pull the trigger if Kevin so much as stumbled.

There was yellow tape around the girl's car on the street—it surprised him to see the Canadian plates. That explained the rounder sound of the few words she'd spoken, the talk around here so flattened down. The tape ran all the way to his front steps, across the wrought-iron railing, as if he were a sorry bit player in an unsolved crime: someone got hurt, some stunned bystander gets caught. And all of it seems drummed up, unlikely to be true.

Even the way the older cop pulls up the green twine like a fishing line and says, "Hey Superman, someone left you a note, it looks like." He takes a torn scrap of paper, tied like a skewed white bow tie in the twine, and holds it out of reach. "We'll just hang on to this for the moment," the officer says. He flattens out the paper somewhat, lets Kevin take a look at the childish scrawl. The old fart's probably thinking it's more bad news on a day gone bust. Wants to goad him into saying something reckless. But it's not bad news, not even close. *Where were you, asshole? I banged at your front door, long time no see. E.*

He has a fleeting thought to clean his place up, make it look like less of a dump in case another girl should drop in without warning. A girl with a bit of a mouth on her. He has to smile at that.

When they get to the police cruiser, Baby Face opens a back door and nudges Kevin inside, keeping his hand cupped around Kevin's head to protect him from banging it on the door frame. He likes the way the cops do that. For tall men, short men, any poor clown too caught up in things to know where he begins or ends. He's seen it so many times in smart-aleck detective shows, but has never quite believed it. Even after they roughed a guy up. They could kick you in the ribs or take a shot at you, but they always protected your head and what little sense you had in it. It's a somewhat tender gesture, he thinks, as if they care about you and what happens next.

MEN SHOUT

"Men shout, that's what they do."

"I know what you mean—across parking lots, so everyone can hear the exchange, witness their sacred brotherhood."

One of the three women in the kitchen lowers her voice to a fake baritone. "Hey, how's it going, buddy? I found that spare part I needed, yeah, that place you told me about."

They all squeal with laughter.

The red-haired one with the supermobile face, her sharp features shifting with every new form of persuasion, says, "Can you imagine doing that, hollering across the street, 'Hey Jill, I'm going in for a few hot dog buns and some hair remover. Catch you later! After my Pap smear with Dr. Salacious, okay?"

Jill, tall with short-cropped black hair, honks in a boisterous way.

"You should get that laugh looked at—"

"I know, I know."

You wouldn't guess she's a top-notch union negotiator, can settle a strike like nobody's business. Or maybe you would—she has tattoos all over her pale Celtic skin, has a way of keeping everything upbeat and still on an even kilter.

"I mean, what's the point of that kind of greeting?" Amanda, the take-charge redhead, asks.

"Marking territory: I know that you know I'm loud and drive a big truck." The blonde sitting on the countertop with her knees clutched to her chest seems surprised by what she has to say.

"And loyalty. Men are big on loyalty."

"And we're not?"

Hammond sticks his head into the kitchen with a cheesy grin as if he's got a secret tucked away in his hamster cheeks. He's got one of those faces that doesn't fit his body; his chubby, childlike features lead you to expect a pudgy man. But he's rail thin in his tight black Levi's, wearing an oversized Hawaiian shirt as a bit of a send-up. He shouts back over his shoulder through the swinging door, "I highly doubt it!"

"I rest my case," Jill says, raising her brows.

"What are you ladies up to? Plotting, gossip, baking a cake?" Hammond asks.

"We're extolling the virtues of the people we love," Amanda says, smirking back at him.

"Above the waist or below?" Hammond asks.

"Above the neck," Amanda cuts in, before he goes further. She's fast off the mark.

"Oooo, sounds serious," Hammond says, deflected, grabbing a beer from the fridge. "Back to the soiree," he says, although it's still afternoon, and they haven't even lit the barbecue yet.

Hammond's a regular at their parties, rarely brings anyone along. He's a tech nerd who's put up snazzy websites for half the people here.

"A lot of men like Hammond"—they all suspect he's gay—"are constantly flirty, have you noticed?" Naomi notes. "It's like they have to try harder to be loved." Again she seems astonished to be sharing a viewpoint. "Imagine if we had to double up on all our gestures, have a different language for our real intimates, kept apart from the daily grind of all the others."

"I think we all do that, no? Keep different sets of friends, show a tamer side to our families. We all have our decoy moves," Jill suggests.

"Oh," Naomi says in soft response. "I suppose that's true."

"I saw him in a cafe the other day, looking very sweet on a woman," Jill says, shrugging. "I've always found him delectable in a kissing-cousin, long-weekend-with-nothing-better-to-do way."

"Don't forget that gorgeous nearly hitched guy at home."

"And I can't forget that he *is* at home, not out with his bunnikins," Jill says, lowering her gaze to a fleck of something on her tiger-print leggings. It sounds like they might have had a nerves-before-wedding tiff.

Amanda leaps into the awkward silence. "Best scene from our first marriages," she offers, tilting her head. "Any takers?" It's easy to see how she puts pressure on a bunch in a boardroom: she's working her way up, up, up in advertising.

"What—now? It's too close, I can't tell; I'm up to my neck in engagement."

"No, I meant our first vows to *honour and obey*. Can you believe we actually said that? Or at least our mothers did—I think we all wrote our first crummy vows, using quotes from Ghandi and *Jonathan Livingston Seagull*, right? It was so avant-garde of us."

"And we didn't keep the promises anyway," Jill says bleakly.

They commit to an odd silence, striking various poses of thinking hard about their first times at the altar. Although the altar was more likely city hall or simply an ad hoc event with folding chairs by a duck-ridden lake.

"We should have just lived together—and then left," Naomi says. "Never married."

"Do you think that would have made a difference—to who we are now?"

"Yeah, maybe." She's still holding her knees tight to her chest. She's drop-dead beautiful—radiant skin, exotic almond eyes, like a model without that sneer they always have—but never seems comfortable in her own skin. Is maybe feeling skittish about the game they're playing.

"Okay, I've got it," Amanda says. "My first marriage. Puppies chewing at his ankles, pulling on his shoelaces and making little growly sounds. The hot breath of the little squat faces, that puppy smell, and our laughing. I mean in that brief moment we were actually together."

"You associate Devlin with a puppy smell?"

"Yeah, sort of oatmealy or milky or something. I guessed it to be an act of kindness, the way he tolerated that litter of twelve in the backyard. I mean, he was such a fucking workaholic, I'd hardly ever seen him with torn jeans on, just sitting on the back steps and being present, you know? He was the one who'd pushed getting married, right off the bat. He'd been head over heels, kissing me all the time. And once we tied the knot, it was fait accompli. He'd break off our lusty shenanigans whenever his boss called. It could be six in the fucking morning and he'd put on his gruff I-work-for-Cadillac-Fairview voice. So I had to read him the riot act one day and say, No talky, no touchy. For a long time before we broke it off, the puppy smell was as close as we got."

"Oh, I didn't know that," Naomi says faintly. "That's sad."

"I know it sounds strange coming from an overachiever like me, but clearly we weren't the best match. Something had to give and neither of us could. Come on, you two. I've unburdened," Amanda says briskly, as if she's just wrapped up a PowerPoint presentation.

"It would have to be a scene away from home…" Jill began. "Let's see. When I caught sight of him leaning toward her at the hockey rink where he was supposed to be coaching? It was just a lean—but you know how you know?"

The others complain loudly. "No adultery stories, puh-leeze."

"No, seriously," Jill insists. "It was a good moment; that's when I knew I wasn't crazy. I began to trust my hunches again, get brave."

"Fair enough."

"You should have shouted across the ice rink, Hey Gus, I'll see you at home—with our son, but without her, right?"

Jill cackles with a note of suppressed vengeance. "A missed opportunity," she says. "Okay, Naomi, spit it out."

"It's surprising," she says slowly, in a trance-like voice. "I thought it would be a scene from the first months, when you're out of your mind and fucking everywhere. But my screen is blank. Like the movie ended and took all the memories and images."

"Cooking together? Him washing your hair tenderly?" Amanda prompts.

"Once I saw him sitting in a park, feeding squirrels. And I played a game—would I like that guy? He seemed thoughtful, kind…"

"But alone."

"Alone, yes," Naomi nodded. "Better with squirrels."

Amanda snorts and gives Naomi a nod of approval. "You're very astute, you know that? Have a good way of putting things. We could use you at the monkey house."

That's what she calls her gig at the big advertising firm.

"I'd be terrible at deadlines," Naomi says from behind her knees. "My sense of time is all whoops-a-daisy and clapping games." She's a preschool teacher, good at make-believe, as she puts it.

The party sounds in the next room are building, while the three women sequestered by the open wine in the kitchen are growing more subdued. There are a few new faces in the mix tonight, including the newly hitched gay couple from next door, one a chef and the other a stand-up comedian, bound to be a hit.

"Have you realized that no one in that gleeful bunch has actually missed us or even pretended to be at a lack?"

"Of beer, just lack of brew," says Jill, as Hammond comes to mind.

"So we come to parties to be needed?" Amanda asks. "Which reminds me, we're supposed to be passing out these smoked salmon dealies so nobody gets too corked." She's munching on one, licking her lips. "They're good, hey?"

"Needed, yes," Naomi says in her soft, puzzled voice, "like a set of tools for opening the universe. They'd be lost without us. Men, I mean."

"She's so poetic. So men are loud in parking lots 'cause they're lost, and we're the tools?"

"We're the tool box…"

Raucous laughter again and Jill slops a little red wine, quickly mops it up from the quartz countertop. The kitchen's been newly renovated; their gritty voices seem to bounce off the subway tiles. Naomi's husband, Phil, did most of the work himself.

"Okay, best scenes from our lives." Amanda's upping the ante in typical ringleader fashion. "Doesn't have to be the very best, but top forty."

"Whoa, that makes us sound like hits from another era."

Jill sings out a few lines from "Bennie and the Jets," and the others join in.

"Hey, hey, hey, watch it with Elton. He *is* the best."

"Okay, here's an example," Amanda says, kicking things off again. "Riding my bike like a maniac down the big hill to the Humber River—that was back in T.O. I'm hurtling along so fast, hair flying. Gravel road, sharp turn at the bottom. I knew it was dangerous, but I'd gotten away with it a zillion times. I think I was trying for disaster, for spectacular attention, and it ended up being just me, taking the risk, over and over, no car of teenage toughs burning rubber to scare me, no one warning me off. There were all these klutz kids getting hurt, but I wasn't one of them. I was clearly a survivor."

"So did you want someone to care more? To stop you?"

"I was an only child and my parents were off in their own little orbits of science and religion. One proving and the other one believing. But I think it was okay. Learning how to handle the skids on my own."

"But you're not on your own, you have Bart."

"Are you kidding? He doesn't save me from anything; he *is* the downhill rush and the risk of crashing." She gives a tight laugh that sounds like a smoker's cough, although she gave that up last year.

"Interesting," Jill says, running her tongue along the rim of her glass. "Okay, here's mine. Kissing Kenny—first love of my life, grade five—in our igloo. Cold air, warm lips, and the pile of snow with a cave in the middle, that's really what it was, starts to melt and sag. It was like a haiku about impermanence."

"So why is that a good blast from the past?"

"Well, it's a bit like Amanda said. I was just feeling the buzz, it was a good, scary moment. I didn't have a clue that he wouldn't speak to me afterwards. 'Cause he was too cool or embarrassed, I guess. I wasn't smart or old enough to know that there'd be other Kennys."

"So, it was the moment before the heartbreak."

"Yeah, when everything's still perfect. And you forget the igloo will melt."

Naomi is taking a long time deciding when her childhood began or ended. "Grassy hollow," she says finally, "as big as a bathtub, beneath a big spreading maple. My den, my lair away from family. All the shouting and crap that went on in that house. I used to go there to read, play possum. To get lost. No one ever came looking or found my hidey-place. I was better off never being discovered. I could make things better just by pretending."

"I can see how that might be a good escape from your shitty childhood," Amanda begins, "but up 'til now? Best of the whole shindig? I mean, you have Phil, and the kids. And the brand new kitchen!" She's gesturing with her arm like a game-show host toward the whoop-de-do prizes.

"Why are we all going back to our childhoods? Have you noticed? Like nothing big has happened since." Jill's trying to deflect Amanda. Sometimes she presses too hard.

"Maybe we're still waiting to be seen for who we are," Naomi says quietly.

"So men shout and women need to be seen?" Amanda's still pushing.

"Need to be *really seen*," Naomi says. "I mean stars wouldn't be stars without the first time you see them—the impossibility of them being there at all—you know what I mean?"

She drops from the countertop and heads down the hall toward the washroom. "I have to pee like a racehorse," she says softly over her shoulder.

"I think she might be depressed," Amanda whispers to Jill. "What do you think?"

"Oh, you know Naomi. She just processes things differently. I think the grassy hollow thing is like the warm-up band for the main act. Like she's working up to the good things."

"I just hope running off to the loo isn't a grassy hollow thing," Amanda says. "I'm worried about her. She's seemed a little distant of late."

There's shouting then, from the front room. It used to be a small, dark living room and now bounces with light under a vaulted ceiling, with French doors opening to the front deck.

"Hey, hey, hey—lay off it, Bart!"

"You don't know what you're fucking talking about!"

Someone bursts through the doorway. Bart's got Hammond by that goofy Hawaiian shirt with all the palm trees and pushes him against the wall.

"Hey man, don't act like I'm some sort of loser. What do you know about it?"

Hammond's looking nonplussed, tries to shrug Bart off. "I don't know anything. Never have. Come on, Bart, loosen up."

Amanda is shaking her head, looking at her husband with a cryptic eye. "Bart, you might want to chill. I mean, what's the big deal here?"

"You stay out of this, Amanda."

Bart's a big guy, strong, plays a mean game of squash. Is used to getting his way and pretending it's everyone else's idea. He owns a luxury yacht business, builds boats for bigwigs like retired hockey players and actors from California who come up to Canada for some sport fishing.

"What? You barge in here, shouting like an idiot, and I have to keep out?"

"Jesus, I need this like a hole in the head," Bart says, dragging Hammond by a clutch of that holiday shirt and heading out the back door. Hammond's allowing himself to be pushed outside, isn't giving Bart any kind of a fight. Is rolling his eyes at the women in passing, trying to diffuse things a little. Or maybe stir them up.

Naomi's come back into the room, looking confused.

"Men shout, that's what they do," Jill says, holding her hands open. She's trying to make light of all the commotion, but she can see the paled face of Naomi, who tends to get upset if there's any tension in the air.

Amanda's looking out the back window, to where Bart's having a heated discussion, apparently all by himself. Hammond's not saying much. "I'm not sticking around to watch this," she says. "It's like a fucking Shakespeare monologue out there. And you know what always happens in the final act. Someone gets stabbed in the back." She's swinging a set of car keys.

"Come on," Jill says, reaching for Amanda's free hand. "It looks like they're sorting it out."

"Yeah, we're stars all right, sought after, looked up to, twinkle, twinkle," Amanda says, as though her grudge is suddenly with Naomi. What she said about stars and men.

Naomi's got a glisten in her eye, like she might burst into tears.

"What—first Bart takes offence at something, and now you? Come on, Amanda, take your own advice and slow it down a bit, okay?" Jill's holding Naomi's hand, squeezing it hard.

But Amanda's gone; one of the French doors out front slams closed and Naomi gasps. It'll be a miracle if there isn't broken glass.

Jill looks toward the backyard. "Jesus, Hammond's been decked. He's lying flat on the grass, holding his face."

Naomi takes a peek and winces. "Where's Bart?" she whispers. "What do we do?"

Jill's already got her hand in the freezer, a bag of ice in her hand. Wraps it in a tea towel. "Come on," she says to Naomi. "Let's check it out."

The side gate's flapping open and Bart's nowhere in sight.

Hammond's splayed on his back, one knee bent, his high-top sneakers giving him the aspect of a crumpled kid in the schoolyard. He opens one eye; the other one's closing fast. He tries to smile up at them.

Jill gently places the ice on his swelling eye.

"Wow, what happened with you guys? You've been friends since forever."

"I felt bad for him, that's all. I said to him, 'Hey, we all make mistakes.' I mean, he looked close to tears. Really broken up. Had just given me the news about Amanda."

"What news?" Naomi and Jill are looking at each other, puzzled.

"About them breaking up. I guess he cheated on her, didn't want my pity for being such a dumb-ass. I mean, let's face it, Amanda will never forgive him. So when I tried to give him a hug, he pushed me away, started screaming at me, and I said, 'It's okay, man.' I mean, men cry too, that's what they do."

Amanda hadn't said a thing; did she even know? Or was she keeping it under wraps? Maybe that's why she'd been on everyone's case.

"Are you feeling okay to stand? Not too shaky? Let's get you inside and figure out if we need to get you to the hospital."

"Naw, I'll be fine," Hammond insists. He does look a little weak-kneed standing up, though. Jill and Naomi each take an elbow and help steady him up the back stairs.

Naomi peeks into the front room; everyone's made a break for the front door, and beyond. She can hear car doors slamming. The party's clearly over.

She takes Hammond to a comfy armchair by the front window.

Phil, who's basketball-player tall, is stooping to pick up the half-empty glasses. "Hey, I'm sorry Hammond. That was totally out of line. Bart, I mean."

He's a forensic nurse, so he takes a quick look at Hammond's cheekbone to make sure it's all in one piece. He sees this kind of face bust-up a lot in prison.

Jill offers to take Hammond home when he's ready.

"It'll build character with that Ned fellow I have waiting for me," she whispers to Naomi. "Twinkle, twinkle," she says. "First star I see tonight…"

Naomi hopes Jill is just pretending to hit on Hammond. That she will only go so far. She knows love is precious and rare enough.

She can see Bart's truck still parked out front. Amanda's behind the wheel, Bart sitting alongside. Except he's not sitting as much as huddled into a man-sized ball, leaning into Amanda's shoulder. And she's patting his back; she's holding him.

TWO BIRDS, ONE STONE

Everything she said used to annoy me. Bad enough that she wanted to *kill two birds with one stone*, that clattering old phrase. But why did she have to say, "That way I can kill two *birdies* with one stone," lending an air of cutesy and cheerful to the act of murder?

I wondered what sort of birds, mulled that over to amuse myself. Or what sorts of hunters—boys with slingshots aiming at carrion-eating crows? Making a few feathers fly among sparrows resolutely chirping on a hedge? I didn't know much about birds, and didn't want to—had learned, at nineteen, all I needed to know from a so-called bird fancier. He was thrilled to find dead ones still largely intact; he put them in the freezer to save for his taxidermy. Stuffed owls and seagulls with blank eyes haunted his dark study. He the old, scruffy professor and I the wary Chaucer student who needed goading toward better grades. His urging usually from behind. The old finagler failed me when I finally had the nerve to cut things off. How naive I'd once been, to believe we all deserve a kind of justice.

I could hear Esther prattle on about her errands, what needed doing after we finished our hike, her voice shrill among the silent trees. She was setting a brisk pace, was the sort to measure the steps taken and calories burned, whereas I'd been thinking of an easy saunter in the woods, a bit of fresh air. But that was Esther; she wasn't given to *being in the moment*, as the yoga types like to say. Everyone's so bloody mindful these days, like Tibetan monks in stretch pants touting pretzel body shapes and a disingenuous calm. I'll admit the idea of letting ourselves off some greater hook sounds like a good deal, but only if you don't have to think about it too hard. That's my take on self-improvement.

I fell back a little when the path narrowed between encroaching underbrush, let Esther go ahead so I didn't have to listen to her. She was so driven, always planning her next move. *Two Birdies, One Stone: A Life of Managed Time* could be a title for her memoir. She was small-time famous for her bug research at the university: how insects interact with decomposing bodies, give you a timeline to the moment of death. Like a clock of ants and bees and beetles ticking backwards. She was considered an expert, had been consulted by film types shooting murder mysteries in Vancouver.

I suppose I envied her, the way she'd carved her own niche in a man's world of unsolved crime. While my enthusiasms tended to fall short, stray off course. Teaching English in Thailand, then a stint at travel writing that had impressed not one publisher, and lately a humdrum position as registrar's assistant at a privileged girls' school. I hadn't exactly *risen, like cream, to the top*, as Esther might say. When she spoke in her trite fashion I could hear echoes of our former selves—how we'd once mocked people acting all too ordinary. Had thought ourselves bound to break all the rules: we were going to dig wells in Africa, free women from prison in Iran, live among the Aboriginal storytellers of the Australian outback. Or at least move to Montreal so we could bone up on our French, change the world from a city with cafes open 'til all hours. Her fallback language reminded me of our mid-century, play-it-safe mothers, that we were both getting on in years, our energies tapering off. Once I'd wanted only the best for her, and for her the best had happened. While I was always just beginning, hesitating, changing direction. And I had begun to despise that in Esther. It was unkind, I know.

At least it wasn't *raining cats and dogs*, or *snowing to beat the band*, and I wasn't *fit as a fiddle*, whatever that means, or *mutton dressed as lamb*, or the sort to *give someone the shirt off my back*, at least there was that. It was misty and cool, with that hint of rusted foliage in the air, the way autumn sneaks up and surprises you. Each time, even after a decent spate of hot weather, you feel cheated.

And then I heard what I later described to police—two years later, but never mind—as a small commotion. A scuffle, the dirt under someone's feet, a grinding or twisting of position. Some small heave-ho. I thought she had fallen, perhaps. The path had roots and rocks that could trip you up. There was a small grunt too—of exertion, or exasperation. Or pain. And when I came around the bend, there in the scratchy sunlight falling between the sweet-smelling pines of a late, dry summer, the browned dead needles—was Esther, strangely crumpled on the earth's floor.

She had a wild look in her eye, unblinking. One arm pulled up over her head, as though grasping at something. Or shielding herself. Her mouth partly open and her torso twisted as though she'd been heading one way and had suddenly changed her mind, gone off in another. And had sunk to her knees in indecision, submitted to something.

"Esther?" I asked. "You all right?"

The forest was silent, a single bird twittering somewhere in the distance.

* * * * *

That surprised look in her eye came back to me recently. How I straightened her body a little, giving her some breathing space. And that's when I saw it, the knife in her back. Its hilt, its heft. A lot of *H* words came to mind with a whoosh sound. Hover. Humming. Howling. Hiatus. Harrowing. Hatchet.

My first impulse was to pull the blade from her cream-coloured jacket—what a shame, I remember thinking, as she'd just bought it—where it had seized upon a rib or wherever it was stuck fast. But I stopped myself from grasping the handle. I'd learned in a first aid course ages ago—when I'd briefly worked in a daycare, and then changed my mind about enabling little hooligans with all their coy wants—that you were to leave the sharp puncturing object in place. If you tore it out in a panic, you could do more harm than good and the poor soul could bleed to death. I remembered that much.

There was very little blood, a mere crimson smear about the shoulder blade, that's all. As if the knife might have glanced off the bone, found a better entry. It occurred to me how little I knew of the human body besides a few nagging sexual ports, gruff throat ailments or ringing ears, a throbbing muscle or two. I scarcely knew where this knife may have landed, what exactly lay at risk directly beneath the skin in Esther's slumped back. It was a well-padded back; she wasn't a skinny little smidgen, so that was probably a good thing, I thought.

I suppose I should have called out for help, shrilly, at the top of my lungs. But it occurred to me that whoever had done this to Esther in my woodsy neighbourhood was not far off. And not behind me, but ahead. So I turned and ran, left Esther in a heap and scurried uphill back to the road, a sudden sharp stitch in my side as if I'd been wounded as well. We hadn't parked at the common parking lot, where there might have been someone to lend a hand. We'd chosen a more remote entry to the huge park, five hundred hectares of bog and ancient trees that acted as a buffer zone between the city and the university. Esther had been proud of her resourcefulness, had noted our single car on the road's verge as if we'd outsmarted a whole lot of wrong-headed trekkers. "Just as I thought," she'd said. "Nobody here."

As I chased up the path I could hear my own blood's rush in my ears. My legs and arms burning in the effort of fleeing to safety, finding help. I was running options through my head; flagging a car down, something. The only cellphone between us was in a pocket on Esther's fallen form. And then it hit me—she had the car keys too. So when I finally reached the bright-blue Mazda— she had washed it that morning, as if for a special occasion—I couldn't hop in, drive anywhere. Find another human being that might be of some use. There are heroes; you read about them every day in the newspaper—I just needed to find one. And fast.

* * * * *

It was early Sunday morning, not a house along this stretch of the park, just a wide swath of wilderness. And barely a car on the road; the several I waved at, frantically, swerved wide of my appeals. I partly blamed Esther, it's true. If she hadn't been such a control freak, hadn't insisted on driving, taking my groceries home first, insisting that I didn't need my backpack—she had a couple of water bottles and that's all we needed, she would drop me off later—I might have been better prepared. At that point I still thought she might be saved.

It was then I heard the sound of a horse's hooves galloping along at a good clip. It wasn't uncommon to come face to face with a horse and rider along these trails: there were hoity-toity stables among old, staid houses at the park's southern margin. Hikers and cyclists were irked by the steaming piles of manure or having to get out of the way of a half-ton beast shambling along, the riders meanwhile complaining of their top-notch mounts getting skittish if we so much as snapped a branch. Then why ride those spooky beasts? I always wondered. But today I was glad to see a big bay coming full tilt round the last bend, the rider leaning forward as if to jump the yellow steel gate not far from the road's verge.

At the last minute she pulled the horse up and off to one side, laughing aloud at her antics. "At one time," she gasped, the horse still wheeling in tight circles, "I would have jumped that gate. I used to think myself immortal."

Even with her helmet on, a few greying hairs strayed round her face, she was pretty in a youthful, reckless way, despite being close in age to myself. We were both of us old enough to know better about our past mistakes.

"Listen," I said to her hoarsely, my mouth gone dry, "a woman's been hurt on the trail—you must have passed her. We need to find someone. I don't have a car, and there's been no one coming along to flag down. So I'm wondering—"

"Where?" the woman asked, her horse rearing up at being reined in. She petted the big nag's neck to calm it. "I didn't see anyone."

"Right at the crook of the path—you know, where it splits off."

"Has she twisted an ankle or something? Had some sort of accident?"

"Accident—no," I said impatiently, as if the woman should know this already. "She's been stabbed."

The woman looked frightened, all the risk of gallop-and-jump gone out of her. "Wha-at?"

"You need to get help. Go back to your stable or find someone along the trails with a phone. It's urgent—may already be too late."

She spun the horse once more on the bark-mulch track and headed back into the woods. I wanted to shout after her, "Look out! He's still in there, the murderer." I figured it had to be a man, had to be murder. And thought to myself bleakly, *We don't want him killing two birds with one stone.*

* * * * *

The horse and rider seemed a sign of sorts. When Tom and I had married, in a secluded clearing in these very parklands, light slanting through the trees, a few friends gathered round on a cool June day, a white horse had appeared. A long-haired woman riding bareback, who went striding slowly in dreamlike fashion through the middle of our vows like a nymph from an old poem.

Of course I didn't want to think of Tom right then. I was still struck by the fact that the rider hadn't seen Esther's body. It might have been shock on my part, but I couldn't recall whether I had moved her fallen form. Placed it somewhere more concealed in the brush just off the beaten path, to keep her assailant at bay, off balance. Wasn't it a crime to further harm a body, even after death? I just couldn't remember the exact sequence of events, that was the problem.

When Tom phoned me at home, weeks later, I was taken aback. Didn't quite know how he'd tracked me down. We hadn't spoken in ages. "Geez, I just read about Esther in the paper. That's so awful," he said. "And the cops don't have a clue as to what happened, who her attacker might have been. It's so weird, 'cause I had just seen her not long before… We'd met for coffee on the fly."

I bristled, because E. had told me it was long over. *Water under the bridge*. I had come to calling her E. in my mind by then, like a nickname or endearment.

It was the way he said *geez* that stayed in my mind. It was a golly-gosh expression that went with the sort of woman who would say *birdies*. As if they might have neatly belonged together.

"Yep," I said curtly, "I knew you two had kept in touch." I almost said *suspected*, but that wouldn't have been right. I did more than suspect—I just *knew*. I finally learned the truth because Esther had told me. Wanted to *clear the decks*, so to speak. Even a bad lie might have served us all better; I could have missed Tom a little longer. Might have trusted E. with the bad news of my estranged heart.

* * * * *

I have become a so-called person of interest in the ongoing investigation. Now the police snoops suspect me, I suppose, which is ridiculous. I can't even halve an apple without cutting myself, am a total klutz in the kitchen. When E. and I lived together for a short time during our student days, she did all the cooking. She could chop things neatly, have dinner ready in a jiffy. She would shoo me out of the way and I always cleaned up later. There was a give-and-take about it, knowing where we stood.

So they're grasping at straws. It's silly to think that I might have a motive because there'd been bad blood between us. The whole Tom thing. I mean there are oodles of betrayals on a daily basis—one could suppose the entire city to be a million wronged lovers seeking vengeance. That doesn't exactly narrow things down to a fine point.

I mean, sure, I had good reason never to speak to E. again, but not to knife her in the back. Come on, I'm the kind of person who shields her eyes at the nasty bits in a slasher movie.

"It takes one to know one," Tom had said to me childishly when I'd called him out on his little dalliance. To date he's never actually admitted it. He simply raised his eyebrows for effect, as in, *You might have seen it coming, darling. You've been there, done that.*

Okay, so I'd met Tom through Esther: they'd been together first. So that means we're all of us thieves, all snitches, all liars, all in love with the wrong people, all liable to be at fault when push comes to shove. In one sense these perusing officers are right: anything's possible. I would have once said quite firmly that E. was least likely to have betrayed me with Tom. She was always claiming her moral high ground. Little did I know.

I can guess what's eating at the cops though. After all this time—and without any other leads—they're trying to wrap things up. So as not to seem dullards, so-called clueless. And the woman last seen with Esther at least gives them a starting point.

Of course I wasn't really *seen* by anyone except the whirlwind rider, who probably thought me a passerby and couldn't *make heads or tails* of what I was saying. I'd no doubt been frantic, *beside myself*, as E. would have said. If I hadn't finally come forward of my own accord, no one would be any the wiser. So I should be given some credit here; I'm one of the victims, lost my oldest friend. Sure, we rubbed each other the wrong way sometimes. But who among us loves without resentment or envy? In that way we were as close as sisters, always competing and fiercely possessive, but bound to share our secrets in the end.

Why hadn't I spoken up sooner?

Well, I said to one of the police fellows—they seemed to be taking turns grilling me—this one with a cocky grin, the acrid smell of cigarettes rising off his casual crewneck sweater, looking as though he were off-duty, which he clearly wasn't. Well, I began again—I had to clear my throat from the tang of smoke coming off the guy—trauma, and disbelief, I said, go on endlessly and take their toll. There's no telling where grief begins or ends. No closure. That's a lot of bumph. And enough time had passed, I added, that I could see the events of that day more clearly. That's why I called the tip line. Because I had a sudden thought occur to me. A small, delicate thing I'd previously forgotten.

I'd walked in a daze along Sixteenth Avenue—no bus stop for quite a stretch. I had barely enough change in my pocket to get home. I started shaking on the bus—someone asked me if I was all right. Tears were streaming down my cheeks and I hadn't even realized. I guess it was starting to hit me, what had happened. But I couldn't exactly blurt out everything to a stranger, could I? There are plenty of nutbars on public transit who talk to themselves in hectic voices and I'd only be considered one of them. So I huddled against a window as the bus lurched along. And then, by some freak coincidence, as I thought then, I saw

Tom's car parked at the next entrance to the parklands bordering the university. A grey, older-model Volvo station wagon, its paint job having lost all its shine. He's long since bought a new set of wheels. But there it was: I should know the car of the man I lived with for seven years, I said to the presiding officers.

"Why did you hop a bus, not stay to see what happened to your friend?"

He made it sound like I'd gone off on impulse, on a shopping spree or something, forgetting all about her. I felt confused by the question.

"Well, I'd trusted the woman on the horse to carry the message, find help—I didn't know what more I could do. There was a giant lull inside me, I don't know what else to call it. The more time that passed, the more overwhelmed I felt, like when the wind gets knocked out of you and you can't make any right sound."

"We've never been able to locate any woman on a horse you might have spoken with. Your friend's body wasn't found until days later."

I was shocked by this news. It seemed all too fitting, given her work in the forensic field, and thereby implausible. A neat procession of bugs invading flesh as though we're all ripened fruit, bound to fall sooner or later. I felt guilty, but not in the way the detectives might have wanted. I'd been hard-hearted about E., and didn't want to go into detail about Tom's hanky-panky—it seemed small potatoes to be moping about my own stung pride, given what had happened to Esther Margaret Harding, renowned entomologist.

"Why didn't you go back?" one of my scrutinizers asked again.

They like to repeat questions to trip you up. I've seen the tactic in countless films where the cops get their culprit. This guy had adopted a different stance from his cohort, was leaning back in his chair, legs crossed at the ankles, hands clasped behind his clean-shaven head—his scalp actually shone under the bright lights—as if he had all day to hear the right answer.

"Are you kidding? I was scared out of my mind—was just a few steps behind her. I mean, it might have been me."

The cops were looking at me like they were starting to get somewhere.

Which only made me blather on, give them a little pep talk. I mean, if it had been some random weirdo with a lust to kill, there would have been other attacks since. And sure, people did stop running there for a time, women especially, but now it's business as usual. People forget; that's what happens.

Except in my case I'm only just starting to remember. Lately a few things have begun to add up. It had to be someone who knew E.'s habitual route, where she normally parked the car. It wasn't a stranger, I insisted.

Fact is, she was supposed to be alone that day. I'd joined her at the last minute, reluctantly. Had been trying to avoid her. But we'd run into each other at the supermarket, and she'd urged me to come along. Was trying to *mend fences*, I suppose. *Life is short*, as she liked to say.

I mentioned the crumpled shopping list I'd found in her pocket. I might have easily taken her phone or keys right then, but my head was all turned around, I couldn't think straight. Leeks, chicken stock, whipping cream and white onions, medium-sized Yukon Gold potatoes. She was so fastidious in some ways, and sloppy in others. Beneath the list of food items she'd neatly printed, she'd added a scribbled note to herself, a last-minute reminder, perhaps: *Call Tom!* They were intending to meet up later, I suppose. No need to write down his number, she knew it by heart.

So it's only just occurred to me that it might have been Tom. That maybe he didn't want to eat her amazing vichyssoise yet again, didn't want her calling him anymore. That maybe she'd become a pest, a liability. You know, like Marilyn Monroe with the Kennedy clan. And when I thought she might have been as unbeguiling, as innocent and childlike, out of her depth, as the breathless blonde film star who came to a bad end, I realized I'd forgiven Esther.

I may have known Tom's wheezing old Volvo by sight, but I sure as hell didn't know what made his heart beat faster. "He keeps things close to his chest," Esther had said to me, wishing me luck in our newly launched marriage. Which made it sound like I'd won him over, her conflicted husband of old. He would entrust to me what he previously hadn't shared, I thought at the time. Talk about love being blind.

She was always generous to a fault, Esther was. "He's like the dark side of the moon," she'd added, an aggrieved look on her face. That was one of her more inspired comments, I think now.

FOR WHAT IT'S WORTH

It might be a sign of things to come, Angie thinks. Good or bad, she can't tell. But she can see a glitch in the usual random pattern of shapes and sizes slouching in window seats, eyes narrowed against the late sun's glare off the water. Tonight is different. It seems scores of men, all unusually tall, have caught the 6:30 ferry from Langdale to Vancouver. She watches them duck, out of habit, while passing through the doorway to the cafeteria smelling of deep-fried everything and stark coffee.

She could tally them up, the distinctively tall men. It would give her something to do besides watching for seals—and finding only deadheads bobbing in the waves. She gets tricked every time, might need new glasses. Or maybe it's just her tendency to see what she wants to see, give herself some clout. She's having no problem catching sight of these men looming heads above everyone else.

It's a safe enough exercise; Mike would not be among them. He had always wanted to be taller; she could sense that a wiry stature inches shy of six feet had pissed him off. She knew he felt that something unlucky had prevented him from growing taller, something dark and corkscrewed down inside himself. A brooding that blew its lid from time to time.

So it might be a kind of therapy. Like passengers conducting business on their laptops or writing in journals, she could pretend a survey of taller-than-Mike men counted for something. Observations cited on May 12, 2002, in case this phenomenon of stretched-out men migrating from one point of land to another was somehow tied to the shifted weather, winter still lurking when things should be blooming. She would take note in qualitative fashion, observing the nature of the situation, not just the numbers. She once did research of that sort for a big pharma company. It paid peanuts and she was shocked when they expected her to skew the facts, make it come out right for their sales promotions. It hasn't made her want to swallow too many pills, even on doctors' orders.

First up, a Massachusetts professor type, six-foot-fourish, maybe a doctor, retired, with his pressed Dockers, a sport fisherman or yacht owner, fond of English setters and the writings of Cheever. He seems American: maybe it's his tone of near complaint speaking to a young woman Angie guesses to be his daughter, his overly proud bearing in his Irish knit sweater, like an ex-army man. Probably has a chi-chi summer home near Gibsons with a great view of the States lying on the horizon, is patriarchal as all get-out at the dinner table, laughing at his own jokes and expecting his Ivy-League family—in terms of getting graduated and married—to chortle along.

Whoa. Tall boy lanky enough for the basketball ranks, six-six at least. He's remaking the sporty-slash-hippie look of the new millenium, orange pants so bright they could have once placed him in the Bhagwan's cult, no questions asked. These days his fleecy, side-zippered numbers say he runs or wants the image of a runner, has paid a few bucks for his high-tech outerwear in some mountain outfitter's store in Whistler: his pants say he eats healthily and doesn't smoke dope. Or doesn't admit to it. His pants say he has a sleek-haired, snowboarding, hiking kind of long-limbed girlfriend, which he does—she's bouncing along in her cross-trainers by his side.

And here comes the next head-in-the-clouds fellow. Even taller than he seems, due to his crouching-while-walking carriage. This is the real-deal hippie leftover, greying beard scarcely spruced up from sipping at lentil soups, or maybe yellowed from roach smoke, woven tunic over a sweater over a T-shirt, the layered I-could-sleep-in-this-and-I-have look. Flared jeans (probably original), socks and sandals—so he's optimistic and adaptive, because there was new snow in the mountains this morning, in early May. He is permanently stooped, might have been shy as a kid from growing so fast, or because he's spent a lot of time thinking about the shrinking universe. He seems to be talking to himself or else tonelessly canting an old Dylan tune while snatching at his beard, looking for someone familiar in the scattered faces on this giant scow.

Giant BC Ferries worker, maybe six-eight, but with a passive just-ignore-me gestalt that eases his size somewhat. He is cleaning out garbage pails with gestures so practised and slow he could be sleeping or in a shaman's trance, his long, long arms descending into the plastic bins and then out, his buzz-cut scalp knowing the exact height of all the doorways on board this ship. When his stiff roached hair touches the door frames he can sense it's time for another haircut.

But the best is still to come. This one is pushing six-nine, and makes more of a statement, too: his faux-suede yellow shirt, his black jeans belted with an embossed silver buckle that's riding as high as the head of a passing Japanese woman. This guy exudes a rough life, glossed over, especially his restless eyes, and his slicked back steel-grey hair suggests he might like country or rockabilly music, has collected most of the old Eagles tunes. She can see that he doesn't defer too often to his wife or sister, whoever she is, a woman with a frizzed purple-grey perm who is walking slightly behind him whenever they pass. And they pass Angie more than once, shouting back and forth at one another. Questions and answers about where they are going to sit, what they need to eat. Coffee? Do you want coffee? Newspaper? Are you sure? No? Apparently not.

There's a whiff of Old Spice that comes with this pair; nobody wears the stuff anymore. It reminds Angie of her long-ago father; he left when she was still young. So she didn't really know him, except for that sharp scent and his shifting eyes whenever her mother nagged him in her tired, grey voice. She still smokes her Black Cat fags, will no doubt croak from cancer, forcing Angie to sit by her bedside and feel sorry. She doesn't want to turn into either of her parents, the escape artist or the woman defeated by her own urging to become someone better. Thinking about her deadbeat family only makes this tallest of tall men more ominous.

He's striding along with a white dog, an Alsatian type, slightly finer in limb, as though a German Shepherd had a quick tryst with a greyhound on the fly. This pale-eyed dog hovers, ghost-like, padding gingerly alongside. Pets travelling with the locals or the gadabout tourists are strictly forbidden on the upper decks. Pets of all kinds, unless they're wearing a snappy red Gore-Tex vest claiming the status of *Hearing Assist Dog*. Which this dog is sporting, although it seems a poor fit, as if the vest might have belonged to a different pooch. The dog is on a short leather lead, and looks absent-minded, following along rather than particularly alert or watchful for its shouty master. It does, however, have enormous satellite-dish ears that could be useful, Angie imagines, for hearing-related emergencies.

She is wondering what those soundless crises might consist of when the loudspeakers on the boat kick in with a blaring hum and static. It's the same ritual warning of mishap they blurt out each and every ferry crossing, comes with a built-in familiarity, like an old friend giving you the same piece of advice over and over. The staff are apparently on their toes for disaster and skilfully trained to lead all those to safety who might be picking their teeth in the sour-smelling washrooms or unabashedly drifting off to sleep. There's always a mention of the lifeboats. And the sound system has that voices-through-fog timbre as though the sailing has already gone off course, the boat soon to be grounded on shoals. Anyone actually listening to this spiel, only the occasional first-time tourist or worrywart of a granny, gets an immediate image of the *Titanic* disaster, some few making it to safety, but most not. Despite the reassurance-slash-warning for unwary passengers of the shambling along *Queen of Surrey*, travellers are told to take note of where the few mysterious lifeboats are located, just in case they have to save themselves.

Is this the kind of emergency for which the white dog is intended? Wouldn't the woman with the already frightened-looking hair be just as handy if the tall man somehow missed the shrill sirens or bells or whatever sound the old, sea-weary ferry would emit if it were suddenly taking on water? Apparently not, says the dog's pacing presence beside the large-striding man. Only this benign-looking white Bambi of a dog could save this fellow.

Angie thinks it's fishy. Didn't she hear the overly tall, under-hearing-privileged man converse quite normally with the woman in the gift shop about the unspringlike weather? About bulbs and compost and straw over the garden beds for the winter? And Angie guesses this otherwise physically capable dude came on board with some big hog of a truck, a camper called a Rambler or Titan plunked on the back, where the white dog could even now be napping, off duty, taking the vibration of the lumbering ship with a grain of salt air and drifting off to sleep.

Angie has a dog tucked away in her old Mustang on the bottom car deck. A black standard poodle named Matisse who is probably careening off the windows of the car, leaving hundreds of love nose prints or going deaf himself from the whine of the giant engines. She was forced to park her car not ten feet away from a door saying *Danger, Keep Out* where the grinding noise was high-pitched and a kind of hot steam was shuddering through an iron grating. She had to leave the windows partly open, which would only make the loud chatter and diesel thrum of the next hour's passage even worse for the poor animal.

It pisses her off that Matisse is caught in some sort of ocean limbo with all the other mutts caught in the death trap below, all the lonesome dogs whining or panting, chewing the car upholstery. She has a hunch the white hearing assist dog might be a scam. A hoax so the odd-bod couple, speaking too loudly as though they might have seen this effect in a made-for-TV movie, could bring their pooch upstairs with them. Plain and simple. There were line jumpers and people who always wanted all the attention in a special ed class. She should know, she's jumped a few queues and taken a few classes for remedial this and that. High school English, then martial arts for self-defence, and recently some motivational drivel that was supposed to improve her chances of success. And for all her awkward silences when asked to review the teacher's gist, there were always those with meaningless questions, as if they hadn't heard a word. The world is full of bullshit, and that's all she's learned and relearned.

She should have thought to go to a doggy outfitter's and have a vest made for Matisse, saying *Unstable Woman Guide Dog*. By now she's probably earned enough of a borderline victim status to make it stick. She has moved back and forth between Victoria and Vancouver and the Sunshine Coast so many times she practically owns shares in BC Ferries. And all because of a man who had stalked her, albeit somewhat romantically at first, with rowboat serenades and banners trailing behind light planes and then on one of those eyesore billboards looking like a trick of falling cards along the highway into Victoria: *Caught you looking, Angie*. They had shared laundry and red wine and arguments together and then he'd run off. At which point she had lingered around his new life a little too long, watching him like a hawk. You could almost say she had stalked him back. So they had found a balance, on and off, of being randomly obsessive. Only briefly had they ever fallen into any category of loving each other. The rest had been taking turns at hating the sight of an ex-lover. Or soon-to-be ex-lover. Because they'd kept having more bouts of rough sex for a while. So they could feel more jealous and jaded when one or the other broke it off. And now it was over.

She knew it was over because Mike had given her flowers. For Valentine's and then her birthday in April. Dead ones. The second time he had hand delivered these delicate, paperlike rust-blossomed bouquets, she had no desire to invite him inside or smash the flowers into his face or send him a nasty note of thanks. Or even get a restraining order. She had just closed the door in his face, softly. Had double, triple locked it. Had gone to give Matisse a big hug for just being there—and for growling. Had turned on some good old Van Morrison and made spaghetti. And shared it with Mattisse, who was a joy to watch eating long slippery noodles. That was it in a nutshell. Nothing more or less. She had a dog now as companion, a daily round of loving which involved walks and rubbing a set of black fuzzy ears, a tried-and-true bond without danger, no shame involved.

Angie has one of her daytime fully awake nightmares. Matisse, bubbles rising from his usually comical face bobbing up against the glass of the Mustang, his eyes surprised by the length of the swim. There is a toddler's car seat churning beside him in the surging water, a limp infant rising up in its harness, a whole slew of carefully caged pets and safety-harnessed children below deck are shrieking and flailing about in the chaos. You're not supposed to leave your kids in the car, but people do so they can run to the john or grab a coffee; they don't want to wake the little scrappers once they've finally drifted off to sleep. And in her disaster dream there's fire, too. There's fire and water, you can have your choice. This very ferry once had the engines stall, then struck a rock while drifting, a fire raging below the dingy fat-smeared kitchens reeking of salt and sugar and clammish chowder. People suffered from smoke inhalation, but she never heard anything about the dogs.

Angie shakes her head free, rouses her calmer self. Matisse is a good swimmer and, with his unruly coat and positive outlook, would be bound to last longer than some in the extreme sport of ferry survival, should the old omnibus start sinking. Still, it makes her mad that of all the dozens of mutts caught in the mayhem on board, the white dog would have the best chance of survival. Should one of the ferry mishaps ever arrive, all those other animals and napping babies and attending mothers, heads back with their eyes closed in their Camrys and Hondas and SUVs, all of them would go down. Except for the white dog. He and his long-legged owner would probably get the first available lifeboat, taking up more than their share of room, the woman somehow left behind. And meanwhile Matisse would be pressing his face against the glass of her Mustang with a "Yo, what's up?" look on his shaggy top-knotted face, dog-paddling furiously.

She thinks again of the drowning baby in her virtual worst-case scenario, who might have been her own, except for the fact that a child, even a fantasy one, requires a father. A fathering sort of man. She had the fleeting thought of a child once, knew it had fastened down in her with the wrong man at the wrong time, which, in hindsight, was all of Mike and always Mike. But the slippery threat of a child had drowned in its own juices before it could grow proper arms and legs. And she still feels equal amounts of sadness and relief, a lot of what-ifs; she can never find a good enough excuse for her regrets.

To date she and Matisse as partners have not yet created anything of substance beyond a collection of plastic chew toys. Not even a fixed address. And the dog treats might not be so fancy for some time to come, since she's just lost her year-long job at a nonprofit. It was only part-time, but it was front line, and she liked it. Felt useful for a change, not used. She would hang out with kids who'd experienced violence, play with them like they had a good day coming to them. Cheer them up. But the funding was cut so she's been laid off. Which makes her nervous as hell, more prone to her daytime terrors. She sometimes dreams herself into a homeless state, living in cardboard under a bridge with Matisse. With shared sunsets and swims and long cold nights together. But then she snaps out of it. She still has a car, yes sir. And sometimes Matisse likes to lick her right ear from the back seat when they stop at intersections. Just to make her protest and laugh. And that's enough, that's all she needs.

Angie is suddenly tired of measuring tall men. She flips through the newspaper—war, war, war, growing poverty here and here on the world map, and corporate theft and drug-running—and she can't make her eyes rest on any one story long enough to even get to the middle, never mind the end. She finally finds a headline that sticks: POLICE DOG JUMPS TO HIS DEATH! It sounds vaguely like a dog suicide but that's not what happened. Seems a cop was trying to pull over a drunk driver who wouldn't stop booting it through intersections, red lights and all. The errant driver finally managed to prang his runaway vehicle against the guard rail of an overpass. The dog, an old pro named Charger, who just happened to be along for the ride after a robbery chase scene, was sent ahead to prevent the drunk driver from fleeing on foot. The Alsatian leapt onto the smashed hood of the car, barking furiously at the man within until the police officer arrived, close behind. When the dog handler shouted for the dog to get down, thanks buddy, it's all cool now, all spoken in quick hand signals and one-word barking back and forth, the valiant creature, all worked up and wanting to get to the driver's side of the crashed vehicle, mistakenly jumped over the railing and onto the highway twenty-five feet below. Instantly mangled. They tried to save poor Charger at the vet's, but no dice.

Angie is welling up just thinking about it. The woman sitting opposite notices her bleary face, leans forward with a tissue, then goes back to shuffling her deck of cards. She smells of fresh nail polish, her eyebrows pencilled in a look of aftershock on a forehead crowded with girlish bangs in a cheap tint of orange-red. The woman has already pushed past fifty, there's no doubt about it, yet she's hanging on to an eerie look of fifteen. Of someone who can't do her makeup.

"Oh, thanks," Angie says to the Kleenex gesture. "I was just reading a sad story in the paper, that's all. No death in the family, nothing like that." Although again Matisse swims in front of her eyes and she feels a sudden need to run down the three flights of stairs to the car below.

"Oh? What about? Don't say our flippin' government, 'cause I don't want to know. Or that on-and-on war in Afghanistan or wherever. I just can't hear any more about that. You know what I mean?" Her eyes are trained on something out at sea, her hands rippling cards more and more quickly.

"No, this is a story about a Vancouver police dog. That jumped by mistake over a guard rail onto the highway below. It just hit me the wrong way, that's all."

"I hadn't heard that," the woman says, looking to Angie for a moment and then back to the dappled Pacific. "It's a shame. Those dogs cost a lot of money to train. And they do a lot of good."

"Exactly," Angie says. "And this dog's been wasted because a drunk didn't have the jam to pull over, thought he could get away."

"I guess it could have been worse," the woman says, shuffling and shuffling. Never laying them out.

"I don't know," Angie says. "Here the dog had all the heart and goodwill in the world, wanted to do the right thing, and this loser of a guy—well, it somehow doesn't seem a fair exchange."

"Whoa, steady now, girl," the woman says, and takes a good long look at Angie this time. Stares hard. She can probably see that her dank hair needs washing, that she lost her makeup bag and can't afford to buy new stuff. So she looks pale and jobless, almost at the end of her rope, which is what she is. "I don't know if you're one of those born-again Buddhists or something," the woman is holding her pack of cards in mid-shuffle, "but it's just a dog, you know?"

"No, I don't know," Angie says, sounding like a kid who's hanging on to her notion of Santa. "This dog, this Charger, he probably saved a few lives, maybe dozens. Not to mention his police officer pal, over and over. So he's worth more in my eyes than some guy who wanted to throw away his own life or trash a few other human beings he didn't give a crap about. You know?"

The woman is blowing her kooky bangs out of her eyes and frowning, shaking her head. She looks out to sea again. "My husband has a salvage business, it's a hard job," she says finally.

"I don't know what that is," Angie says, but she's thinking that Matisse is worth three Mikes and ten jerks she hasn't even met yet. That there is a balance somewhere, a pattern, and she is just finding it. She is sticking to the dog's side of the story, no matter what. She's made her mind up and that's that.

"My husband? He goes along the shoreline after a big wind or storm and picks up logs that have left the booms the barges are towing, have drifted ashore. He and a friend grab a few big ones off the beaches and tie them together and take them to the mills and sell them for whatever they can get."

"So what's your point? Is there a dog in this story?" Angie asks, none too graciously.

"Sometimes my husband—Bill's his name—is dog-tired."

Angie snorts at the pun.

"Oh, I guess that's funny," the woman says. But she's not smiling widely. She's not smiling at all. "Well, anyway, he's mostly so tired his bones hurt from jumping in and out of the boat and climbing along the rocky shore in his hip waders and hauling on ropes and all of that. He's getting too old for that stuff. And yet he's afraid to stop. He has a few pints sometimes at the pub after work, likes to drive home on the coast road he knows like the back of his hand."

Angie sighs. She's done the same thing more than once or twice, tossing back a few and then hitting the road. But she sure wouldn't admit it to a stranger, like she's proud of it. She makes a wry face and hears the loudspeaker do the smeary-voiced welcome to Horseshoe Bay, urging people to get back to their cars and pronto.

"Well, I'm going to go kiss my dog now," Angie says. "He's been cooped up down below."

They both rise stiffly and walk to the garbage bin, take turns throwing in their paper coffee cups.

"I still don't think a dog, even a superdog, is equal to a man's life. Any man's life," the woman insists.

Angie doesn't want to get into it. The woman's obviously not a big fan of dogs and is sticking up for her husband, and that's okay. They walk silently side by side in the same direction, toward the back of the ship. There's a sudden smell of Old Spice approaching from behind. The towering man with the white dog surges past them. There's no woman with him now. The dog looks woefully over its shoulder at Angie as if to say, *Excuse me, I'm sorry. I'm just a prop in this story.*

The woman with the lifted eyebrows and the fire engine–red bangs whispers to Angie, as if they're old school chums and bound to say something slightly nasty about someone on this voyage, "Hey, what about you? If you're such a dog lover, what's your take on this deal? Myself, I think the dog's a fake, or at least the guy with him, and he's no more deaf than you or me."

The tall man with the white dog swings his head around to look at the women behind him, almost as if he heard something. His eyes flicker. And then he remembers to keep walking straight ahead.

FOUND TO BE MISSING

She's had the ringing in her ears for days now. A faint timpani, a shivering of the senses, as if she might be as hollowed by hunger and fear as that boy on Mount Seymour, the one who's gone missing. She imagines you probably start hearing things out of desperation, something like the whirring of a giant hummingbird's wings that might be an approaching helicopter—or the pale thrumming of death itself. If she and Max were in that sorry state, holed up in some gully or gulch, she wonders who would trudge off on their last legs to find help—it's said to be a bad idea. Or, having stayed put and exhausted all means of making a teensy fire, having finally lost hope, who would be the first to gnaw on the other's bones? Best not to go there.

The tragedy for the lost boy, Iris figures, has something to do with how close he is to being found. She's said so to Max, that it's sadder if he's being missed by inches than by miles. She keeps picturing the intended rescuers moving closer and closer, but never catching sight of him, never hearing his faint cries for help. It's like that childhood game, where someone shouts, "Warm!" or "Cold, freezing cold!" when you're trying to find the one who's hidden, sometimes right under your nose. The boy needs someone making a ruckus on his behalf, pointing the way. She wants to share this with Max, but some days she's not sure whether Max even had a childhood.

"Don't remember that one, Iris," he would say dismissively. He's simply not the red light, green light, hopscotch type.

It's Iris who likes games, who buys the Lotto 6/49 tickets, noting when they've missed by only three numbers, Max reminding her that only getting *all* the right numbers counts. Then we'd finally be agreeing on something and be a hell of a lot richer, all in the same blink of an eye, he says. He laughs at the idea of the two of them sharing an insight; it's as unlikely, he thinks, as having ten million dollars drop into their laps. Max doesn't trust in gambling, has some safe investments in a few blue-chip stocks, but Iris is what he calls hopelessly hopeful.

She doesn't like to be reminded of their slim chances. They share so little beyond this brief time in the mornings actually facing each other and speaking. Everything between them is measured, withheld, watched carefully even when given. Of late the lost hiker has given them reason to exchange words, share a subtle mood of anticipation. Their sudden keen involvement in the story keeps track of their whereabouts, draws them together, like an impending death in the family. When you've been waiting for any change in a limbo of wait-and-see, even a quick end to things can bring relief.

But Iris is trying to defy the odds. She thinks the boy might still turn up. "It's like when you lose your car keys and they're right where you left them," Iris says to Max about the boy.

"Except no one left him on a mountainside with a snowstorm on the way, Iris. No one misplaced him," Max says, with that note of sarcasm drifting into a deep-timbred voice you would otherwise trust. Even in a snowstorm. "The reason you can never find things, Iris... well, I'd say it's a matter of losing your mind, not your keys. Or your purse. Or where did you put that tea towel you just had in your hand?" He does that thing where he combines a cough with a laugh, as though the thought of Iris and all her foolishness causes him to feel good and bad all at once.

"I meant the boy, the boy losing his way, not seeing something as plain as the path downhill," she murmurs. There is resentment in her voice. She tries to imagine obvious things the boy might have missed about his life and then longed for frantically in the dark and the cold—perhaps a loyal, known-her-since-high-school girlfriend, a favourite Cowichan sweater, an angular cat he adored. And then she tries to imagine losing Max.

Even when he's not at home, she can hear his voice, what he would say, how he would correct her vision; he's always looking over her shoulder. It gives her some satisfaction to picture calling the police, reporting a man missing from her kitchen table. Insisting that yes, he has existed in a long marriage at this address, but no, his even-paced voice is no longer tallying up the facts about a lost hiker.

"He's not here this morning reading the Mount Seymour story," she would repeat calmly a second time. What else could she say? That she missed his accusations, his readiness to pounce on her feelings?

"I know he was restless, wanted to buy land, had his eye on a couple of weird properties in the middle of nowhere. I remember thinking, Is he turning into a recluse? Will we ever see other people? As it is, we hardly go out anymore."

If it sounded too much like complaining, not grieving, she would soften her tone. "It seemed he was driven to keep looking for a place away from all our old connections. If the ad said, *Remote access, no services*, he'd call."

The constable (he would be RCMP, young, somewhat baffled) would be making notes. He would have dropped by the house to investigate her muffled plea for help. She would be smoothing the front of her shirt, thinking herself untidy, unprepared to be the centre of attention. And enjoying that, despite Max's mysterious disappearance.

"I don't know, maybe the land was just an excuse. He's always been obstinate like that, wants what he can't have, doesn't enjoy what he does have," she would add, though it might seem disloyal.

The idea that she's always wanted to initiate canoodling—as Max calls any sort of lovemaking between them—and doesn't know how, doesn't dare, would flicker through her head as it often does, coming out of nowhere. Perhaps because the officer gives her a glance that shows interest in her as a woman, but more so because he is listening to her intently. As though he needs to hear her version of the story. To Iris that is more seductive than a boyish hairline or the generous sweep of a man's shoulders.

"He drinks," she might admit, depending on her mood, "Cabernet Sauvignon, good Merlot, his favourite brands from California." She doesn't know how that would help them find him. It's just so others could picture him, know him a little as she does. The way he'd acted right before she lost him. That he would tipple a few glasses to improve his dour moods, but that the wine often made him more abrasive.

His routine? His regular habits? Yes, certainly, she can answer that. It might be hard to describe to a young fellow, probably irresponsible as hell outside of his uniform, how habituated a man of Max's age could become. To explain Max's rituals, she would risk laughter or disbelief.

Every morning Max will typically look out to their North Vancouver deck noticing whether the paper boy—who is really a man with a flimsy part-time job and an old beater for a car—has flung the *Sun* neatly onto the top step; Max will grumble when the fellow has missed his mark. Sometimes Iris slips outside in her bare feet and nudges the furled newspaper higher up: it seems to affect Max's day when it's misplaced. *She* has to live with him, after all, not the poor guy throwing papers every which way.

Once she rebelled, she remembers, and nudged the paper onto the sour, wet lawn, the newsprint falling apart later in Max's fingers, making him furious. She found an article in that very paper, once it had dried out somewhat, on the anger index in middle-aged men who might be slightly overweight and leaning toward a crabby retirement. Max fit the profile perfectly, the impatience in traffic, in bank lineups, the way he flared up at Iris sometimes. And he's already taken early retirement, is at home full-time now, which doesn't really help either of them.

Every morning he spreads the paper out on the kitchen table where Iris typically perches, ill at ease. She sips her coffee carefully—sometimes the sound of her wet lips on the cup's edge, her small swallows bother him. She will feel the fickle moments of winter sun on her face, shift about in her chair, wanting, most mornings, to be back under the covers. Couldn't they read the paper in bed? she asked him once. He seemed to think that ranked them high in the kinky-sex department, gave her a long lecture on the sanctity of his newspaper ritual; one can't turn the pages properly in bed, one can't sip coffee without spilling, and on and on. "Plus you," he said, looking at her with a father-knows-best glance over his bifocals, "only read parts, then get twitchy."

Let's face it, they're not good at this start-of-the-day thing. While Max attacks the paper methodically, perusing headlines, licking his fingers to flip through the sports and business pages at a purposeful pace, she's a sporadic browser, taking random looks at the classifieds, clothing ads, movie reviews, rarely finding a headline that draws her in. Occasionally she really latches onto a story, worrying it until she's resolved something to herself. For a time it was anything about the rape camps in Bosnia: she murmured the most horrible atrocities out loud, so that Max would somehow be involved too. "One woman, one hundred and fifty times. Her thirteen-year-old daughter too. These men are husbands, brothers. I can't understand it. Can you, Max?" She would well up, her face growing bleary with despair.

She expects Max to comfort her when she's shaken by the truth. She can feel the terrible thing reported as though it's happening to her — can feel her tongue turning purple if hundreds of seniors are trapped in gargoyled old apartments in a Paris heat wave. But Max grows impatient with bad news, accuses her of only reading desperate stories as if to entrap him.

"Human interest, Max. Not desperate. You know, the three great themes — " She pauses, can't quite remember the lessons of Greek drama, but feels pressed into defending herself. "All stories have something to do with love, envy and pride, remember?" It sounds wrong, but what the hell does Max know.

Max will typically show more emotion at a ball thrown wide on a football field or his MacBlo stocks edging down than at the dark side of human nature revealed. Like the mother who put her car into neutral and let her young sons slide down a boat ramp while strapped in to their car seats, their frantic cries soon underwater, leaving no sign of her ever having given birth at all.

Admitting in her confession, cool and relentless as that lake water, that she felt released from a great burden. Iris circled around that grim story for days.

"Me, I prefer human disinterest," Max says, whenever Iris tries to shake him up. But the photo of the two small boys really got to him: Iris could tell by his wry face, as though something in his coffee was curdling. "Look what happens when people start obsessing and losing a grip—Jesus, all that woman in Tennessee needed was a good babysitter."

It startled Iris when Max started reading bits and pieces of the Mount Seymour story aloud. As if he was taken by this event and needed to share it with her. Perhaps because it was closer to home and seemed more likely: Max himself had hiked in these mountains not long ago. For the first couple of days she relished the new-found connection between them, believing it was bound to be brief because it was so uncharacteristic of Max. Now, almost five days into the search for the student—he attends a local university—Max has her full attention. "And now for the continuing saga of the young man lost on Mount Seymour," he will typically say in his deep, somewhat gravelly voice, with a pointed look over his glasses in her direction. At least it sparks some conversation, albeit the typical sparring between them.

"It's funny, he didn't leave until three o'clock. A witness saw him trekking up the east slope then. That's an odd time to set out; he was an experienced hiker, after all. Maybe an hour of light left then."

"Maybe he didn't intend to come back. Maybe he wanted to disappear."

She knows it's one of the things that disturbs Max about her—her so-called flights of fancy. He doesn't understand what makes her leave the ground. "You're flying solo on this one," he will typically say to her. He might be able to talk to her if she wouldn't always veer off topics, is the implication. As though his reluctance to enter into conversations with her is somehow her fault.

He scoffs sarcastically, his mouth full of dry toast. "Have you wanted to do that? Leave the car and head God knows where, looking good in your latest outfit, having people worry about you?"

She *looks good*, at least he grants her that. Although the *latest outfit* part is surely a dig at her spending of money. Or perhaps at her vanity.

"It's like the old hiding-behind-the-corner-postbox trick," she says, trying not to mind his sneering. "I did that once as a kid. Even negative attention was better than none at all. My parents scolding me later only showed me they cared."

Iris is stirring her cup of coffee in a figure-eight pattern with her spoon, as though performing a rite of alchemy, as if she might transform French roast into gold between them. "Sometimes you have to push the plot a little. Remind people that you exist. Sometimes you just have to remind yourself."

Max is tipping back in his chair, looking up at the mountain. They can barely see one face of Seymour from a small wedge of their breakfast nook in their east-facing kitchen. From this vantage point they can imagine the small figure setting off, looking unlike any sort of imminent tragedy. At least until he was found to be missing, one of those media phrases Iris loves for its unintended irony.

"Found to be missing," Iris murmurs softly, framing Max's profile with her hands, as though holding her old Pentax steady against her eye. The colour in Max's face is bleached out by the raw morning light, the dark background of the coastal mountains seeming more in focus than the indistinct figure of her husband.

Iris took a photography course once, snapped a few good pictures. Her instructor had said so. Mostly of people, strangers caught in animated discourse or laughter, their bodies arrested in some vulnerable midpoint between gestures. Caught without self-awareness sharing food at cafes or running headlong to catch buses. For a time she had a fleeting notion she might make a professional pastime of it, those serendipitous shots at weddings or family reunions that are more memorable than the posed portraits. But she didn't understand the mechanics, Max reminded her once too often. She finally abandoned the expensive lenses and filters he'd bought to prod her toward her fascination with images. It seemed he was taking over and she couldn't see things the way she wanted.

It's the same thing all over again with the stuck-on-a-mountain story. Iris pays little attention to fresh inches of fallen snow or how hard a wind might be blowing off the Pacific. She looks for other signs in the boy's life—the fact that she calls him a boy already gives a great deal away. Hers is the Jungian approach, she told Max one day, mispronouncing the famous psychologist's name like in *young at heart*. Didn't matter to Max; he called the man a sex addict. Mistook Jung for Freud and didn't understand why Iris believed an all-too-famous shrink with all of his gobbledygook might have anything to do with this misadventure.

"It's got nothing to do with sex, Max," she said. "It has to do with coincidence. What we see as an accident." Of course she didn't have much to go on, relying on sketchy reports by the media. When the missing boy's older brother flew in from

Toronto, acting as wary spokesman for their mother who was already a nervous wreck, Iris wondered aloud, "So where's his father? They haven't mentioned his father."

She imagines the father having died in an earlier family mishap or having flown the coop, been a real scoundrel, the elder son having to pitch in and help his family financially. The younger brother, the hiker, staying home and staying in school to keep his mother company, give her some comfort. He is only now resisting, running away from the task of feeding his family emotionally, knowing his mother will resent his moving away. Of course he's angry: it makes sense. But not angry enough to confront her. In order to lessen the blow he's had to invent a near-tragic demise before he can even begin his own life. Perhaps he's already fallen in love with a svelte poli-sci student with long, swinging hair who wants him to move to Peru.

If Iris were to share this projected storyline with Max he would only give her one of his looks that said she'd missed the mark. Max looks at the obvious facts, listens faithfully to the weather reports, even tuning in to the marine forecast, noting the visibility closing in, the winds changing, the intent look on his face left over from his Chris-Craft days.

He sold the boat last year; too much work, he said. It seemed a metaphor of sorts when he lost a measure of passion for the boat he had named *Blue Iris*. Iris took it personally, and actually misses the dreamlike rhythm of slapping on coats of varnish when Max murmurs things like "Seas at four-foot moderate. Winds twenty-five knots and gusting from the northwest." She supposes their hours on the boat didn't merely maintain the mahogany, what Max reverently called the brightwork, but made their time together shine with a rich patina as well. Now, to hide her nostalgia, she mimics him when he pipes up in his old captaining fashion, calls him the ancient mariner. He looks plainly annoyed when she crosses her arms hard over her chest, pushing out her stomach muscles and dropping her voice for effect, "If it doesn't look good at Point Atkinson, it doesn't look good for that poor boy on Seymour."

Iris is surprised how compelling Max's curiosity has become regarding the lost hiker. He's even phoned the rescue patrollers, pretending variously to be a ready volunteer or a frantic friend of the family, just to get more details. He is really quite convincing, the way he changes the timbre and expression in his voice. She has never before seen him act with any deceit, witnessed any theatrical bent in the man she married. Or seen him display any tendencies toward gambling, for that matter. Suddenly he's fascinated with the odds against finding the hapless boy, despite the young fellow being a capable outdoorsman, dressed for the changeable west coast weather in early December, his brother vouching for his previous experience on rough, steep terrain. She thinks Max might be toying with his usual reliance on life being a series of equations with ready answers. That he is doubting himself.

His response to any predicament has always been how obvious everything is, as though she can't see an answer as plain as the Mensa puzzles he insists on showing her every Saturday morning. Last weekend's square inside a circle stymied him for a moment, and so did her off-the-cuff response that the answer was eight, she could see it.

"It's not something you get a gut feeling for, or estimate, Iris," he said too patiently, as though teaching a toddler a fine motor skill the child would grow into eventually. "It's a mathematical calculation, the square's diagonal being 1.414 times the diameter of the circle. I took this in my first engineering courses, I should know this," he said with a telltale edge to his voice.

He was shocked when the answer was eight.

"I have a good sense of serendipity," she said breezily, meaning to say telepathy. Her gifts were not his, and he couldn't see that. She could actually sense Max thinking about the number eight in his mind.

It was clear she'd caught him off guard. That's happened more than once since they've been sharing the news of the search on Mount Seymour. She can sense a shift in power between them, as though she might have an inkling about the lost trekker hidden in her, as part of her own landscape. A landscape Max doesn't understand as well as the jagged treeline on the North Shore Mountains rising behind their home, as the fickle air currents among those peaks that can send a rescue chopper spiralling into an abyss. He has started to feel uneasy in their exercise of hypothesis. After all this time searching, the fog distorting vision and voices and shrouding any likely swirls of smoke from a signal fire, rescuers are unable to report even one small finding that might lead miraculously to a despairing hiker. Not even a snapped twig. Even the search-and-rescue dog looks listless on the TV broadcast, apparently ashamed of his luckless snuffling over the cold, desolate mountainside.

Max is unsurprised to find Iris hopeful, nonetheless. That's the woman he's grown to know, always fired with an energy that makes his view seem too stoic or sensible. She is still slim, he has to grant her that, but Iris knows she wears a softer outline now, like the blurred photo of a woman caught in motion. What Iris used to call an art shot during her darkroom phase. She assumes it's come from twenty years of matching her stride to Max's, careful to avoid the struggle that might have made her image more distinct, separate from his own. She's sensed for a long time that she doesn't cut the same sharp profile that used to give him shivers—that's how he once put it—whenever she approached. But in the last few days she's started to come back into focus again, defining herself against the premonition of loss on the mountain. There's something at stake in finding the boy. And she likes the sensation, wants Max to remember the old feeling of being unnerved by her, feeling short of breath and out of control.

"Did you hear that, Iris? They say sound's not even travelling one hundred metres. Heard that on the CBC evening news." Max is a firm believer that anything reported on the CBC comes close to the gospel truth. "Jesus, unless they trip on him, and soon..." Max's voice trails off. He pours the bottle of Cabernet more frequently, grows silent.

Iris is wearing a wistful smile, her head tipped back against the sofa. She's wondering whether Max could hear *her* at one hundred metres. Often he doesn't listen when they're side by side, having her tell most stories twice like the storybook character Jacob Two-Two, hoping for at least an irritated response the second time round. And if he hasn't heard her in these many years, what would he know that could save her in a pinch? Would he know her habit of criss-crossing her own path, running amok like a startled rabbit? She's the sort to forget where she parked the car, to look surprised when coming out of a store. She does best when brushing up against things that stir her senses; she'll remember the sweet smell of candy on the fingers of a crying child or the face of a beautiful young woman selling bangles on the street, a series of shifting impressions that are always moving, always leaving her lost. Afterwards, she won't remember where the heck she was, whether on Robson Street or at the Lonsdale Quay, when she found herself distracted by the swirling world.

Max wouldn't be aware of her tendency to stray; he's always walking ahead in their strolls to the supermarket, will seldom look back to her on their walks in Lynn Canyon with their chuffy little terrier. Sometimes she's afraid to lose sight of him around the next street corner or along some heavily wooded path, afraid she might lose her bearings. That he might not notice her absence or turn back to find her. Even then, he would only berate her, never let her hear the end of it.

He will scarcely wait for her even in the uphill climb of their lovemaking. Just when her heart starts to race, the steep ascent strangely compelling, like climbing a soft set of stairs faster and faster, the risers lifting her up, up, up, as long as she can keep her balance, hang on to something—just then Max will grow quiet, stroke her absent-mindedly, fall soundly asleep.

She suspects a misadventure in hiking would end much as their passion leaves off, with her heady sensation, a feeling of total abandonment. A feeling that she has never been anything but entirely alone. Max would be hard-pressed to find clues as to her whereabouts. Does he have any sense of her aversion to evergreens, even now, when it's nearly Christmas? Maybe it's something left over from childhood, like the way her normally patient father seemed to struggle with the tree, curse and swear until he had it right. But she thinks it's the sort of tree itself—all prickly and sappy. She likes wider trees with softer leaves that aren't so dark and spired, unforgiving. But last year Max dragged home an especially big blue spruce, put a small pine in the front foyer as well. She thought at the time he did it to annoy her, but it's worse than that—he just doesn't know her that well.

Does he sense her fear of being trapped beneath things, of being caught inside a spider's web? Even something that flimsy makes her panic: she's more than slightly claustrophobic. Even their configuration in bed would relay this to him, if he's been paying attention, how she will hold her breath, squirm out from under his heavy arms, his shelter feeling like leaning, like dead weight.

"If you were lost up there?" Max startles her with the impression of reading her mind, at least in part. "You'd probably leave a trail of receipts."

It's true she shops and overshops, buying soft lambswool sweaters in styles with a cowl neck or three-quarter sleeves, in maroon and aquamarine, finding she's already bought similar ones and since forgotten. She sees it as a kind of shoring up process, decisions she can make over and over and nobody wanting to change her mind. There's the zing of the cash register and it's all hers—Max doesn't come into it. He doesn't really notice what she wears. It would give him some difficulty in describing her to rescuers. "She must have been wearing the red sweater," he would say, trying to take charge, and then be confused as to what was actually missing from her wardrobe. That's the kind of detail that could lose her, Iris thinks.

"Maybe the whole thing's a set-up: the young man seen walking up the mountainside late in a winter afternoon, his abandoned car found next morning, a school friend noticing his absence only after allowing him getaway time."

"Why do you do that, Iris? Why do you tamper, insist your dream world on a real, tangible scene where people are measuring temperature and snowfall, charting distance, trying to keep choppers in the air for hundreds of dollars an hour. It's a huge operation..." He's seemingly run out of accusatory breath. Adds only, "Who do you think is paying for all this?"

It is then they hear the bad news. Max and Iris stiffen, almost simultaneously. They are sitting at far ends of the old floral couch where they typically wait for any details on the late-night newscast. The rescue party, swollen now to almost a hundred volunteers, is threatening to give up the search. The next day will be the last chance for the boy to be found unless the weather changes.

It's a sobering thought for Max and Iris. They've started to live their days according to an apparently failed search-and-rescue mission. After five days they were hopeful, the two of them, for simply a body. Max thinking it would be a case of recovery, the boy found dead, and Iris still believing there was a whisper of a chance.

Iris says quietly, "At the point we start watching, we know so little, don't you think? Outsiders know so little of what really goes on."

She still believes it has something to do with the boy's emotional life, although she doesn't say this aloud. Several possibilities come to mind—she imagines a case of unrequited love, this getting himself lost business is his ballad beneath the balcony, saying, Notice me! I'm hot for you! Together we could change the world! He's still young, after all.

It's equally possible that his long-time steady girlfriend (the high school sweetheart he's been taking for granted) has been unfaithful. It's conceivable she finally said *Screw you!* by taking another lover who treats her like a gift, yes sir, who celebrates her. It's hard to say whether the hiker is feeling sorry about this situation or simply sorry for himself. Anyway, it starts out innocently enough, he feels miserable, wants to go for a walk to clear his head, finds trekking up a mountain better than finishing off a bottle of Scotch, better than makeup sex with this long-familiar girl—that was one of the problems, after all—and then it hits him; why return? He likes this high, this feeling of cool anxiety, the sharp thinness of the air, the warm burning in his legs. He can't stop climbing, won't let himself turn back even after the sun falls behind the dark curtain of spiky trees. He's been absorbed into the rockfaces, the blackness, the cold—he's been absolved, leaving his debts behind.

Iris is thinking of kindness, concern, perhaps even curiosity, all the intangible things owed to loved ones. But to make it easier for Max, she puts it in his terms.

"Maybe he owed a heap of money, maybe he embezzled funds." From his brother's take on it, the mother has struggled to put him through school, has her whole life invested in the kid. There's never yet been any mention of a father. And maybe the boy's resentful about this lack, or simply following in his errant father's footsteps. The hiker seems like an earnest, tree-hugging type, with no family fortune to look forward to, no clear way to pay off his student loans beyond a lot of hard work, so she adds, "How about from a non-profit foundation? Where he volunteered out of the goodness of his heart—until he had a change of heart. Did something rash, like his black sheep of a father."

"Iris, get serious. They haven't ever spoken about the kid's father."

"Exactly," she breaks in.

"And hikers don't embezzle money. Especially biology majors—wasn't that what he was?" They both notice he's used the past tense for the first time. That he's given up hope. "They drive Volkswagen vans, grow beards, change their own oil." He chuckles at this, makes a vague motion with his hand in his lap.

"You lack imagination," she says, her lips pursed against his crude remark.

"If I have too little, you have more than your share, Iris," he throws back. "You should give some away for Christmas this year." He makes that clearing-his-pipes sound that resembles throat cancer in that movie with William Hurt, if you didn't know better. The fact is, and that is the point Max doesn't get, they *don't* know better.

It could be game over for either one of them at any time. Last year she had a lump in her breast. It all turned out fine but she didn't share any of her worry with Max. Didn't want him pooh-poohing her concern that they might carve up her breasts, which would give Max the willies; he'd never look at her again. But he's no better off, sits on his prostate all day. Since his retirement Max has led a very sedentary life: when he suffers back pain his doctor chides him on his computer nerd posture. Poised for hours above a keyboard like that, his shoulder blades drawn out like wings. And despite his low cholesterol, Max could sprout those wings tomorrow.

If he suddenly takes a notion to climb Mount Seymour, joining the volunteers on the last day, his heart stammering on some steep ascent, would Iris smell his Irish Spring aftershave when temperatures fell below zero? Would she find him where he'd plunked himself down to regain his breath, knees curled to his chest like a small child, needing her rescue? Would he even think to call out her name in distress? She thinks not; pride would prevent him. Like the screwdriver thing, when she wanted to help him connect the new cable for the VCR and he pushed her aside. He was capable, he said. It seems he always grows more capable with her next to him, eager to pitch in. In that sense it's probably better that she stay behind, at home, never joining the search party, allowing him to save himself. If they aren't careful, she imagines, plumping the cushions where Max has left a heavy imprint, a puffed-up proudness will kill both of them sooner or later. One at a time—she can't picture it happening together, kaboom, kaboom, dead as doornails, like you always hear about old lovebirds. Their deaths will be lonely and apart.

"You coming?" Max's voice sounds distant from the bedroom. He's already undressed, entombed in the duvet.

Would she ever have the courage to call out to him in a desperate moment of needing help, when she's afraid, even now, of him watching her undress? The odd thing is that she's equally anxious that he'll fall asleep before she can slip into her flannel nightie and lie beside him. Close, but not too close. At the ready, as it were. Just in case.

Her greatest fear on a lonely mountainside with night falling would probably still be that she was not *desirable* enough. Would Max want to risk life and limb searching for her? Not simply out of loyalty—he is a decent man, she knows—but in order to regain her presence in his bed, by his side. Would there be enough passion to warrant the search?

After all, he had never really looked for her, had found her by chance. She was absorbed in a book, licking a spoon clean of blueberry yogourt in the cafeteria between classes, third year of university, right before she dropped out. He said she was cute, that her tongue turned him on, but he didn't know then what he knows now: her dappled freckling in the sun, her sour faces when his words sting. He didn't know she'd remain in a kind of limbo, suspended, a few courses short of the sociology degree she'd intended, a few miscarriages shy of the family they'd once wanted.

So now, should he find her a second time, beating back bushes, using grappling hooks and waterproof torches, would she reward his efforts? Simply by existing, by being alive? "We were both hooked, right from the start," he used to say, liking the sound of his good fortune in fishing. She's afraid that the woman he once considered a trophy, he might now, years later, simply throw back. Saying, breasts too small, hips out of season. Her acute awareness of some things, innate innocence of others, sure signs of an endangered species.

She can't bear the thought of being a disappointment on the late-night news. "I passed right by her," he might say. "Couldn't see her for looking." And Max not seeming too torn up about it, either.

It might be easier at this point to remain lost to him forever, to keep her identity concealed and thereby somewhat intact. She alone privy to her limbs growing colder as the rescue squad falls back down the dark mountain, Max in front, directing them with clear instructions. Assuring them that the ring around the moon means rain in eighteen hours. Her death would be one of misunderstanding, of her own silence.

She slips shyly under the covers, afraid to waken him. Would her last thoughts on that mountainside be of Max, or just another of her fantasies? In her favourite recurring one of late, she's holding the attention of young men, still boys really. (They are not going to take advantage of her; they are not going to take charge—that's important.) They have a fresh quality, not yet jaded, might be the age of the lost hiker with all of life still ahead of him—he hasn't even really become a man—and she's willing to believe she is not too old for these boys to watch, to touch gingerly in their minds, as though she is a luminous painting, a vision they can hold for themselves. They believe she is lovely, tug at their tender parts, will be affected by her sweet attentions to her body when they choose lovers. Like the haunting music and sad bedroom scenes of that wistful movie *Summer of '42*, she will have touched them forever.

In the way she imagines it tonight there is a measure of distance and safety in the way they stand on shore, the boys, while she floats lightly in the rowboat, out of reach. That way she can tempt them with her knees up in the boat that holds her afloat, the water lapping softly at the hull. Their eyes will shine at the loosely draped shawl, the dark colours flecked with gold, the tassels tempting her nipples, she pulling the shawl up slowly between her legs. The winding of silk long enough to lie around her shoulders, droop down softly over her breasts, the rowing endless and patient, leaving smooth, soft ripples in her wake, as though she has forever to remind them of a woman's desire. Like a trick of light shimmering on the water, the boys may imagine that she straddles the varnished oar the colour of honey, pushing the smooth round wood that sits comfortably in her palm's grip, the boat spinning softly in circles.

She knows the boys on the shore would fade, the shoreline itself would fall away, if she had the courage to take Max along in the boat, have him row for her, and just lie back. She opens her eyes hard against the dark, lets the idea take hold of her—if she could believe that Max might yet find her pleasing, a bit of good fortune, they would both be more content. That's the last thing she remembers on the fifth day of the search.

* * * * *

On day six, after nearly a week of rain and sleet and winds of such strength as to warn small craft off the waters of the Georgia Strait, the weather seems calmer; there are brief, swirling moments of sun caught in a racing sky of burly clouds. Iris is dressed in the white terrycloth robe Max gave her for Christmas the year before. She is leaning her breasts comfortably on her crossed arms at the table's edge, the gown gaping slightly, her bare feet curled over one another for warmth on the cold tile floor.

She is reviewing the dream she had in the night. "You might as well put up a sign," she shouted to Max, her voice sounding stretched and strained as though she were fighting to be heard against the roaring of high winds. He turned with a sour look on his face, not a trace of the sympathy she wanted. He raised a huge sign then, the letters spelling *Mount Seymour*, although she could see behind Max forever, the land flat and treeless. Where she had grown up in Saskatchewan had been like that. For a moment she thought she was back in her own childhood, safe. But Max was mocking her, as usual. Now she lived with him, surrounded by mountains—even in her grade school geography texts they had scared her. You either took to them or they took you prisoner. Loomed over you.

But if Max thought she wouldn't notice, she could see beneath the black letters shouting *Mount Seymour* the faint outlines of a smaller script: she had to trace the writing with her fingers to decipher the words. *Caution—horses*. What were caution horses, she wondered. Did they turn away in some painting, like Colville figures with blank, dark faces and windswept manes? No, it was something less ominous, more hopeful, she remembered thinking in her deep, swirling sleep. She thought she could see them moving slowly, like phantom beasts, their long-legged silhouettes gathering on a plateau at dusk. There were a great number of horses, it seemed to her, but she wasn't afraid. Their hoof beats sank into her like the soft thrilling of her own heart.

"I had a dream with herds of horses last night," she says to Max, on impulse.

"Horses mean sex," he replies. "I saw it on a talk show."

It's a concession to her, to admit he watched a talk show. To even mention sex. He knows, after all, it will trigger a series of actions in her head: she will wriggle somewhere, stretch, yawn, get a hint of colour in her cheeks, expect something. For some reason he is stooping to her, sweetly.

Max takes an obvious peek down the front of her bathrobe. "A herd probably means lots of sex," he says. "Or good sex."

Iris deflects his glance by pulling up the edges of her white robe. "I remember playing horses with my cousin Jill. She always wanted me to be the prancing horse so that she could have her way. Tell me what to do."

There is no response from Max, only the sound of the newspaper thumping perfectly on the top step. Iris tiptoes out to the deck in her bare feet to retrieve the furled sheaf of hectic stories, all the jibes at politicians and sports heroics, conflicting weather predictions, ads for new cars and pricey condos. Always obituaries too. Still, the world seems full of new sun, the air warmer than yesterday. Today is perfect weather for reclaiming what's been missing, for relief. She is almost certain they will find the boy.

"Any news yet?" she asks, typically leaving the headlines for Max. So it can be his discovery, then his turning toward her.

Max spreads the paper out, his voice taking on that measured distance from events that leaves him free and clear. "Headless body recovered," he reads out slowly, and then falls silent, mouthing only occasional words aloud. "Snow bridge. They think he fell through a snow bridge into Cascade Creek."

"They don't think there was any, what's the word I want—foul play?" Vaguely connected sequences from old cops-and-robbers shows crowd into Iris's head: a murder scene in stark black and white without witnesses, only hunches. There are shadowy figures, dark cigar-stained voices, abrupt telephone calls, the line left buzzing.

"Log boom," he says, in his resonant could-have-been-a-newscaster voice. "They think he got caught up somewhere in the flow of water, squeezed between some big trees, or a rock, that's how he was…"

Iris is puzzled, her face shifting with each new question. "But why would…" she begins, her breath caught somewhere between in and out.

"Why is the sky blue, Iris?" Max says, moving on to the sports and business sections, thereby closing the subject of the hiker.

"Have they ruled out bears?" Iris begins again, wanting to hold fast to a small part of that broken boy. A feeling of panic rises in her and leaves her with a sensation of floating, numb and cold, like that body. She can scarcely feel the outline of her face, the hair twisting softly at the nape of her neck. As in the stories she's heard of phantom limbs, she imagines only the faint stirring or memory of a head, perhaps a habitual craning of the neck stump or the sensation of eyes flickering where not even empty sockets remain.

"Iris," Max says reprovingly, "it's over. Finished. They'll never know for sure."

For Max, it's obvious; finding the body is somehow enough. "Nah, bears would have snacked on the rest of the body," he adds as afterthought.

"I knew it," Iris says softly. "I just knew it."

"What did you know, Iris? Just what was that?" Max asks absent-mindedly.

"It's not a simple story, Max. None of it's simple and straightforward. And it's not finished, either. I can feel it in my bones."

Max ignores her. He brushes his lips with a finger, flips to the financial pages, traces the stock listings.

"If I were his mother, or just a friend of the boy's, or even if I was just Iris, I know I'd want to find the head."

Max looks up at her, startled, the corners of his eyes looking strained and bloodshot. As though the search has worn him out. "That's what *she* said, his mother, that she wanted the search party to keep looking, to find the head. That she couldn't rest until it was found. Bloody ghoulish, if you ask me."

"She wants the story, Max. Not the head. She wants to know what happened, that's all."

"Thanks for sharing, Iris," Max says, giving her the fleeting brush of dry lips on her cheek that signals his habitual retreat to his study down the hall.

Looking for only a head is a whole different ball game, as Max would say. The story will have shrunk, been relegated to some back page by the time someone comes across the empty lantern of a head, months or years from now. Perhaps another trekker slightly off the trail catching sight of the skull. She imagines the discovery like an anthropological find, a rare vase or shard of pottery. The boy's death posing new or unusual questions about survival in the late twentieth century, about technology or religion, the fruitless search for his return marking a learning curve of human compassion or care. Some will use scientific terms in describing the hiker's head, will measure the brightness of the bone, the marks of force or erosion, discussing the effects of foraging animals, cold weather, marvelling at the cleansing of time. Poets or high school students struck by other subtleties of love or loss may write more obliquely of a solitary young man meeting his awkward fate. His mother will simply weep.

Iris walks softly like a sleepwalker from the bright kitchen to the study in perpetual twilight, a small screen buzzing with figures and Max hunched intently in his favourite oak chair, as though he might lift off into the ether of the world wide web. This has been going on a long time, the padding in the leather seat tufting out, the arms of the chair worn from years of Max leaning back, suspended in thought.

Iris drops her head down and hovers over his right shoulder. She hears him breathing quietly, like a man drifting in some meditative state produced by the pinpricks of light on the monitor, the clicking of his fingers on the keyboard. Something in Iris reaches out like the widespread arms of a rescue party entering dense brush, retracing steps they've already taken a hundred times in the hope they've missed something.

"Think of yourself as lost, Max," she says softly, not quite believing her own voice. "And it's my job to find you. I'm looking for a man with a body and a head, and that other thing they never talk about in newspaper stories."

Max pulls her around to sit on his lap, one arm comfortably around her waist, his other hand teasing the edge of the robe on her thighs.

"I meant the heart, Max. A man's heart."

Max's eyes flash in warm recognition and he tips his head back, laughing hard. She can feel his raucous heartbeat overlapping with her own, insistent and familiar.

Iris gasps from their shared sense of surprise, catches her breath. "We must be out of shape. Maybe we haven't been laughing enough. Listen to us wheezing—it's as though *we've* been climbing that mountain," she says.

"And hoping for the best," he agrees. His arms are still holding her.

It makes her feel good to hear him say in his usual wry manner, "It's all uphill from here."

THE READING

"I would like to say how thrilled I am to be here—to be given this opportunity. I've been coming to this festival since I was a girl, and to be among such gifted colleagues and mentors, really, I'm speechless..."

If only, he thought. What was she—pushing twenty-five? She *was* still a child, for Christ's sake. With her quasi-commando getup, those big clodhopper boots and leggings, long, sloppy skirt, that defiant makeup of dark-shadowed eyes and purpled lips so common in magazines, sweet young things with small, quaking voices wanting to look tough and capable—of warding off men, of dealing with life's annoyances.

He was blocking her out, thinking of a dream he'd had the previous night. Of sleeping with a bear—not in the bed with him—but in the room, close by. And of trying to measure whether, if the bear woke up, he would have time to escape its raking claws or gnawing teeth; so he stayed where he was, scarcely breathing, afraid to rouse the bear...

Perhaps the dream meant he was tired. Weary of this business of hosting young pipsqueaks with nothing to say for themselves—dear God, they hadn't lived long enough, that was the problem. Had some simpering little thesis from years of yawning through grad school wrapped up in book covers, and now considered themselves full-fledged writers. And his nod, on a small festival stage with a well-worn Asian carpet and intimate-seeming lighting, faux-leather armchairs arranged just so for the cozy interview, Booker Prize nominees wandering about signing books—that didn't help matters. He was through with listening to the tentative readings of so-called emerging writers, their hemming and hawing afterwards to inane questions—always the same ones—How did you come to writing? *Oh, I knew from quite a young age, when my teacher in the third grade...* Did you have to research the scenes involving firefighters? They seemed so true to life. *Yes, well, um, I mean, I lived in the bush one summer, in Canada, with a horde of tree planters, among scads of small forest fires, had quite an eye-opening time of it, yada, yada.*

Who cared what sleek ironies of youth she might describe, what trysts she might have had with a transient tree planter, or firefighter, or architect in Dubai? He had a sudden savage urge to bring this woman spouting gratitudes—to her family, to her editor, to her partner, that special loving man (if, indeed, with a name like Cade, he was a he and not a she, you never knew these days)—to her senses, wanted to tighten up her generous world view a notch.

They were seated, obliquely facing both the audience and each other, mics pinned to lapels. In her case a bohemian top, in torn denim, half off her shoulders, the mic lollygagging nicely near her ample bosom. She was searching for her place in the text, flipping pages, then found a pale-pink Post-it—ah, there was her starting point. She nodded coyly to the audience beyond the stage lighting, as if to say, *Silly me, ready now.* Just the pink page marker and how she had forgotten it, or hesitated to begin—or perhaps the whole thing was just a performance, an affectation—outraged him.

"Let me give your readers a brief introduction to your work," he began. And she smiled at him, tilting her head, thinking herself to be in good hands. He was one of the best, had worked for the BBC for eons and now worked the festival circuit because it meant lots of perks: travel, good food, wining and dining with the literary movers and shakers, hard-nosed agents and scathing critics not afraid to say what they thought. They were an amusing bunch, always somewhat at one another's throats, seething with various jealousies and affronts.

"It was my impression," he began, "and correct me if I'm wrong, when reading your stories—because it's not really a novel, is it, but a loosely linked collection of vignettes or scenarios—that the world in your work is the glazed glance of pop culture, brief notoriety—people bouncing off of bright surfaces, even off one another." Here he gave a salacious laugh that a few easily convinced audience members instantly mimicked. "It seemed to me that your characters have landed in a rather shallow social milieu, and that they find themselves too good for its disappointments. That they deserve better lovers, better employers, better restaurants, even better epiphanies..."

Her mauve-shadowed eyes had half closed, as if in reflection, or perhaps great restraint. She seemed to be studying the phony art deco lamp on the small table between them as she considered her response.

"Yes, I think we have the ambition, when we're young, to make a better place of it—it's a bit like having a bad"—she paused here, wanting to perhaps use the word *interview* and thinking better of it—"encounter and coming out the other side with a new awareness, new weapons, if that's what's required. It's a bit like the scene in my novel"—she paused again, the word *novel* dangling in mid-air—"of a woman throwing knives. She wasn't born that way; she had to learn how to throw sharp, pointed blades into an obdurate surface. So that they would stick in place."

Now she was looking at him with that same gestalt of daggers in her eyes, a stray soft tendril of hair by her cheek grown spiky and sharp, or so it seemed.

Touché, he thought. So she did have some spark to her.

"You explore some themes," he began again, "that might risk seeming overworked, that have been done before. The experience of manipulation, as portrayed by physical or psychological abuse, for example. These stories seem to come from ideas"—he knew this to be the weakest starting point for fiction, often unconvincing, a common trap for young writers—"an inner manifesto, if you will, more than personal points of departure. As in, I'm guessing you weren't a supermodel"—there was an awkward silence in the room then, the you-could-hear-a-pin-drop sort, as if he'd insulted her beauty along with her powers of invention—"and haven't been locked in the trunk of a car by terrorists; I'm guessing that you had to research these contexts"—to death, he wanted to add; although, to be fair, he hadn't read her fiction that carefully, had been busy the night before dreaming of bears.

She fastened a look on him so dark, all the blonde highlights in her hair, gleaned from living a healthy life outdoors with tree planters, no doubt, seemed to vanish, and he thought she might in fact have a terrorist cousin or two in the mix of family.

"Life is short and fiction is long," she said then, her lips thinned to a straight line from here to there. "Although it often seems the other way around, time in a novel being compressed, and the reading time of a story just a matter of days, while real life, in real years, seems to fall away at an even faster rate than flipped pages. First you're published and pleased about that—and then you're old and half of what you wanted to say is still a secret, even to yourself, and the other half fallen on deaf ears."

He was somewhat taken aback, felt a prickle on his scalp that was not quite raised hackles, but close. She had clearly done her homework, for he had once published a not-very-good novel. What was it, forty years ago?

He could sense the audience being more attentive than usual, no rustling of programs or coughing, as if they were intent on having a disaster unfold before them. Like some sort of TV reality show, the cruelty of literary survival and sparring temperaments about to come unravelled on public display. The room fairly sizzled with tension, someone in the audience gasping, as if the twosome in the prickly limelight might actually come to fisticuffs.

Not so thrilled now, are you? he felt like admonishing the girl. Not sitting so pretty now, are you, my sweet? Not with an old curmudgeon testing your mettle. And you giving back as good as you're getting.

He let her read then—it seemed a truce of sorts—from that pink-noted starting point. She rose to the lectern and shook back her long hair—he hated that gesture in young women, performed as if a dishevelled, come-hither look might better seduce listeners than words—but she stood squarely facing the room, no wobbling from foot to foot as some did. And didn't do a half-bad job, he had to admit: she didn't overly dramatize as some writers do, as though they're theatre students in mid-audition, and she didn't speak too quickly or drop her voice, as if ashamed, as others do. Her voice was jagged, somewhat desperate sounding, or secretive, which suited the darkness of the text, and she seemed to fall into the trance of the language and movement in the story, into a proper breathing and pacing. And he noticed then, her face half in shadow at the podium, that she might have the haunted look of a woman who had once denied herself food, of flesh settling over bones reluctantly, like a contest of wills, health and womanhood finally winning out over stick thin and angry. So maybe he was wrong, and she had been imprisoned at one time, by an eating disorder or by runway modelling, by some sort of enemy capture-and-release.

She read from the scene of the woman throwing knives. And planning vengeance on a never quite explained tormentor. She didn't immediately say thank you when she was done, as some mistakenly do; she let a telling silence fall over the room before the applause started up, as if there had been a great many in the darkness beyond the stage affected by the telling. The clapping went on, he thought, a little too long, as if the audience had forgotten his role entirely. He was intended to summarize, thank sponsors, but didn't quite know when to break into the on-and-on smacking of hands in approval. Some silly twit even shouting out "Bravo!" as if he were at the opera.

His throat felt thickened, and his mouth dry, the applause seeming to roar in his ears. Water, that's what he needed before he stood up—he was parched, that's what was wrong. But his arm was suddenly flailing and he failed to reach the water pitcher, fell forward in his chair toward the reeling floor. There was a chafing tightness in his chest, as though he were bound round and round with a straitjacket, the sounds and lights of the room receding to a dull pounding of something like a distant drum.

In the dream the bear stirred. And it went first to the body of the woman sleeping next to him—he'd forgotten that part, how this woman, unfamiliar to him, and young, half his age, just a girl, really, might need his help or he might need hers. The bear snorted and sniffed, then seemed to make a conscious decision to spare her, that was the strangest thing. Then reared up before him and made a terrible gnashing sound, like the wind in a winter storm splitting branches or teeth tearing at bone.

And suddenly she was all over him, the young writer, loosening his shirt, calling out for a doctor, an ambulance, pressing down with the heels of her hands onto his staggered heart—"One-and, two-and, three-and, four-and, five—" She was counting in that jagged voice, rocking back and forth on her feet in those commando boots, and he wanted to say then: You read like a real trooper, will probably make it in the long run; in fact this may be your crowning moment toward a future stardom—no one will ever forget you helping a dying man, being so brave under the lights, this strength of yours an unexpected tenderness in a tedious world.

SMALL GLORY

It's been three years and not quite what he'd expected. He'd thought his decisions would matter when time ran out and he was hoping to hell he could drop a man or get some fool in a desperate mood to drop his weapon or his guard. He'd been prepared for a lot of hoping and dropping. Bad things that might eat at him later. And he's ended up just keeping the peace.

Most days he's on his own: it's a small town, nothing much going on beyond break-ins at summer cottages, cars stolen for a lark, some kid on the lam from home or the occasional small drug bust. Oh yeah, and domestic squabbles—he said, she said, and the charges always get dropped. He moves away or she changes her mind, or the deadbeat dad finally agrees to pay up for the kid's expenses. And every day he's on the beat he has to write reports, each tedious detail of what make and model of abandoned vehicle, what the punk said in his own defence, what time the disturbance took place at a party house when neighbours complained.

The thing is, he likes working solo, doesn't mind that he hasn't been shot at countless times by street kids or low-life mobsters with nothing to lose, which is what happens in the bigger cities. You get burned out there too, but in a different way. So it surprised him when Shelley packed up and moved back to

Toronto. It's a pretty decent life up here for raising the kids she had wanted and he hadn't been sure about. A hokey town, sure, but far enough north of the sprawl to be at ease with its own shortcomings; people know him and trust him somewhat with their troubles.

But Shelley told him he was bound to die alone and she wasn't sticking around to watch it happen. Which didn't make a lot of sense but she was crying and upset when she said it. He tried to change her mind but she turned away, holding her shoulders high against him.

"We'll see," she said. But he doubts she'll be back.

He doesn't understand the risk she saw in loving him. Most times he hasn't had to do more than touch his hand to his holster, enter a room with a gritty look of authority to make a few rough characters toe the line. Fact is, he's still waiting—for that one time that changes all the odds, something has to give, it's here and now and no other choice.

"Look at Goff," he'd said to Shelley at the head honcho's retirement party, "he's kept himself smart and safe all this time." He knew Shelley liked the officer who'd taken the young guys under his wing. Had shown them how to handle a gun, hence his nickname—so a firearm didn't "go-off" in some knee-jerk reaction.

"It's the having to do it that gets you any little bit of glory," Goff always said. "When you pull your gun, you have a little talk with yourself, you rhyme off a little ditty you've made up—it's a goddamn prayer, really—to give you pause, keep on top of things. And don't share your shoot words with anyone—they're yours to keep shiny and sharp."

Of course he'd told Shelley his little mantra. About the street he grew up on as a kid, how he used to run toward the white-trunked trees—a stand of paper birch where the road petered out—when he was in trouble, needed some time to figure things out. He told her how the leaves would rustle in the wind, and late in the year turn to gold, be the last to fall before winter. He told her because that's what love forces you to do, spend your good luck in the middle of some dark night.

Today being summer, when tourists hit town and things heat up with petty crime and random complaints of "I heard a noise," he's feeling grateful for his shift cruising the back streets. He likes the gut feel of the work whenever he gets a hunch something might be out of whack. He takes a sudden turn off the main highway passing the sleepy Muskoka town, the sun-blistered sign promising a population of six thousand, nothing much changed since the draft dodgers came up here twenty years back and a few hippies started having kids and growing weed, and not in that order. Sometimes, on these dusty roads leading nowhere, he finds a thing or two worth writing up later at the office.

And bingo, almost as soon as he's had that thought, he turns onto a road he knows to be a dead end, down near the river. There's a car parked halfway into the ditch, an old Volkswagen Beetle from way back when, and nobody at home. Or wait a minute, somebody at home all right—what strikes him as a young girl's lanky leg slung oddly over the steering wheel. He feels his chest tighten, and cuts the engine, coasts to a stop a few car lengths behind, half-hidden by a wide-spreading oak.

The leg wiggles a bit, so it's not dead. He's thinking a tryst in the car and hopes it's a willing one. He'll give it a minute, see what happens, whether anyone straightens up, puts on clothes in a hurry. But the leg stays there.

So he closes his door softly and starts the walk up to the car from an angle that's in the blind spot from the driver's seat. Those dinky side mirrors not giving much away.

He doesn't hear voices, not a single sound as he scuffs his boots lightly through the dust. He's about ten feet from the little hunchbacked car when there's a sudden movement and the girl's sitting up behind the wheel. Adjusting something in her lap, it looks like, as he leans forward and sees that she's alone.

"Everything all right here?" he asks, seeing the girl smirk a little sideways at him. She's winding down the window with a screechy sound of old rubber against the glass. Has a nervous habit of looking away and then back again, like she can't quite believe another human being walked up, unannounced.

"Oh yeah," she chirps quickly. She's wearing shortie shorts, not much else, a halter top skewed to one side, and she's straightening it as best she can.

"I'm just thinking there's got to be a reason you parked here— meeting someone?"

"Nope," she says, doing that half smile up at him, and then looking away. Maybe eye contact doesn't run in her family.

"Could I see your driver's licence, miss, and your registration?"

"Oh yeah, sure," she says, leaning across the car to a small, stiff glovebox. He tries not to look, her skinny little bottom half exposed for all the world to see.

She hands him the paperwork, and he's sure he smells it, the tang of girl on her hands. She was parked here lovin' herself up a bit. Oh God, he thinks, here's one for the books.

"Haven't been driving long," he says, and now he's smiling, like he's sharing her secret.

"Naw," she says, "there's nowhere to go, but it gets me outta the house."

He doesn't bite, doesn't want to ask about the home front.

"Drive to school?" he asks. She gives him a sneering look, as in, *It's summer, you idiot*, and he adds, "I mean when it's not the holidays."

"I stopped going, wasn't doing too well," she says, dropping her chin so he can hardly hear her.

"So you have a job now—something to keep you busy?"

"Nope," she says, "I was working at a gas station, you know, selling the pop and stuff, and then the guy started hitting on me so I was outta there."

There are only two gas stations in town, and he knows it's possible, what she's saying.

"Well, you can't give up," he says. He's getting antsy; there's too much talking and he wants it cut and dried. She did something, he counsels her and lets her off some hook—the world gets slightly better.

"Aren't you going to search me?" she asks, right out of the blue. "I mean, for drugs. Isn't that what you're worried about?"

"You don't strike me as the druggie type," he says, trying to hide his surprise at her outburst. Wanting to make her innocent as all get-out.

"My boyfriend is," she says, lifting one coy eyebrow at him. She's daring him to take it further and he looks over his shoulder just in case her skanky pal is somewhere cutting a deal in the woods, her pretty little antics just a way of setting him up.

He wonders if she even has a boyfriend, is maybe making things up to sound older with a lot going on. There isn't a stitch of makeup on her, rare for a girl her age if she's seeing boys.

"Maybe you need a new boyfriend, Cassandra," he says, handing back her licence. She's barely sixteen and on the verge of things getting out of hand. He'd been warned about this, right from the start—a lot of people treading water, and you can't do a thing to help them.

"Nobody calls me Cassandra," she says, biting her lip. "Unless I'm in trouble."

"Not with me, you're not. Not yet," he says, smiling. He can't help himself from asking, "Problems at home?"

"Just freaked-out family stuff. A lot of shouting and slaps in the head out of nowhere, I didn't do a thing... you know."

He thinks he might know her folks. The dad's been out of work for some time. And the mom's a real looker, a little bit tarty and on the prowl.

"I still think, a new boyfriend, new job—you've got choices, you're a smart girl."

She's looking up at him for the first time. Twisting strands of baby-fine blonde hair by her face, her grey eyes flinty with gold specks of grit. She's just young enough—or old enough, he can't decide which—to change a few things for herself.

He remembers the toddler he brought to the cop shop a couple of years ago. He'd found the kid—maybe three or so—in a frosty ditch, ducking away from his cruiser like a skittish animal when he pulled up. Running like blazes when he'd asked, "Hey little guy, you lost?" There wasn't a house for miles, early Sunday morning. The child had peed his pants and stunk of it, was cold and shivering when he finally cornered him and grabbed him round the waist. And the kid had a shiner to boot.

They drove up and down for a bit, him asking the kid as gently as he could, "You live up there?" pointing in one direction, then,

"Is this close to your house?" pointing down a side street. But the child said nothing, his eyes round and staring.

At the station they sat him on a defunct telephone book and the woman on dispatch took one look at the tyke, then shook her head. "He's been in here before," she said. "His folks live up the street a couple of miles. They're probably hungover."

Vespers, their name was, and the place was straight out of a movie set, one window boarded up with plywood, snow blown into a couple of wrecked cars in the yard. Although he banged on the front door good and hard, nobody came to answer.

The dad showed up a few hours later, still reeling with a hard-bitten look of hangover, and said, "I want my kid back."

"We have to fill out a bit of paperwork," he'd said to the guy, who looked old enough to be the boy's grandfather. Maybe it was the drinking, killing him before his time.

And in the end they had to give the kid back; the social workers said the situation wasn't bad enough to warrant lifting the child from his home, putting him into foster care. He remembers thinking it was easier to rescue a dog from a bad setting than a small, helpless human.

He's looking back at the girl now, and saying, "You know, you have to be careful on a back road. What you do and how you pay attention. You're at risk, you know that."

They both know what he's talking about now, and she's got that half-smeared smile on her face.

"I've been here before," she says. "Lots of times. Used to go down to the river as a kid. So I know who comes here—nobody."

He wants to laugh at her now, outright. Pull the cover off her little bit of sass.

"Well it only takes once," he says, "to be in real trouble. And you should have seen it coming."

"Summer I was ten there was somebody," she continues, "a farmer who'd brought two horses, those big kind that work the fields, down to the river. And he had the mare stand knee deep in the water, and his helper held her in the stream while the stallion, well, you know, gave her a ride…"

Again he's surprised that she's so full of talk, and still somehow childlike.

"The farmer got mad at me for being there: I was poking a long branch into the water and out again, making little plopping sounds. He acted like he owned the river, said, 'You have to be quiet there, girl. They've got their business to do.'" She's mimicked the farmer's growly tone, which is funny to hear, but he keeps himself from laughing, lets her finish.

"The mare was terrified, made these awful screaming sounds—but she couldn't move, or she'd lose her footing on the wet stones—I was practically bawling my eyes out."

"The farmer must have seen my face and felt bad. He said to me, after they'd washed the mare off, 'We have to do it this way. Otherwise she might kick the stallion, hurt him real bad. But she'll like having the foal alongside. They always do.'"

"But the younger guy liked being rough, he liked every bit of it. He was yanking the rope on the skittish mare to hold her steady, and gave me a look in passing, you know, *that* kind of a look…"

The scene, the way she tells it and breaks off, her face clouding, strikes him as real. It's something she hasn't been able to forget. He believes her. And thinks she probably has a load of crap at home to contend with. And for a moment he has the realization that small towns might be ugly, not pretty and quaint, somehow untarnished.

And then he sees the boy. Running out of the woods, as if something or someone might be chasing him. Screaming so hard and shaking his head from side to side, it seems he might come unglued, arms and legs flailing as if fighting a monstrous net and he's tangled in it, can't get free. The boy stops, sways on his feet when he sees the cop car. And then he comes running full tilt again, screaming God knows what—he can't make out a single syllable.

But there's a glint in the sun that hits him right as he unsnaps his holster. He's looking along the dark edge of the gun barrel to a point on the horizon, the boy drawing closer.

"Do something," the girl whispers fiercely. "He's got a knife. And he's crazy when he's like this." She's eased herself out of the car, is hovering close behind him, all her sweet talk gone to rust.

"Get back," he hisses at her. "Crouch down behind the cruiser."

The kid is right off his rocker, off his meds, or on them… Who knows? And there might be someone on his tail coming out of the trees behind him. Somewhere in the distance he can hear a siren chirping—or maybe it's a bird in the cottonwoods sounding an alarm.

"Hold up there, son!" he shouts in the direction of the boy hurtling his way. "Drop what you've got in your hand and nobody's going to get hurt!" His voice sounds hoarse, though he means to be calm and in charge.

The boy is still shrieking so hard he probably didn't hear the warning. Or didn't want to.

He can hear tatters now of what the kid's screeching, something about "all the Jesus Christ fucking lies"—he's feeling betrayed, that much is clear. It might be about the girl or some deal gone wrong, or he might just be mad at the dizzying way the world turns—and none of it really matters. They're in the thick of it now, all three.

"White trees and you're home," he mutters to himself as the boy grows larger. The kid's hefty, older than the girl. "White trees, white trees, white trees," he repeats, to steel his nerve, keep his aim pure. He can hear the leaves stir softly, see a flashing of light among the white whispering trees.

The boy's face is ragged with the thing that's sweeping through him, still yelling his fool head off and lurching to one side, as the gun wavers a little.

ACKNOWLEDGEMENTS

A friend once said to me, "you've done that; now do something else." Short fiction is an exercise in that wry advice: it forces a writer toward endings that help us move on. Many thanks to the whole crew at Nightwood for their resilience in these difficult times of distance and patience, and for their fine tuning of my fictions, Emma Skagen, Annie Boyar and, of course, Silas White, for his first look and astute recommendations beyond.

I am grateful to those enthusiasts for my work who gave me rapport and listening, made me feel recognized in the hunt for the right words, among them Andreas Schroeder, Sharon Brown, Genni Gunn, Frank Hook, Heidi Greco, Joe Baker, Helen Tervo, Hal Wake, Larry and Karola Stinson, Cindy and Ian Dayneswood, and my gung-ho writing group, Robert, Cindy, Chris and Tess. Much gratitude, as ever, to my daughter, Alexis, for her presence in shoring me up, for her laughter and longing for better, better, best. Thanks as well to her partner, Ian Homer, for his friends' takes on my poems and for driving old cars made to last.

The title story of this collection, "Sunday Drive to Gun Club Road," was shortlisted for the Carter V. Cooper Award and will appear in the *CVC9* anthology in 2021. An earlier version of "Found to Be Missing" was published in *Prairie Fire* and won a nod from the late Matt Cohen.

PHOTO CREDIT: KAT WAHAMAA

ABOUT THE AUTHOR

Marion Quednau has won numerous awards for her fiction and poetry, including a National Magazine Award and the CBC Poetry Prize People's Choice Award. Her novel *The Butterfly Chair* won the SmithBooks/*Books in Canada* First Novel Award and was described by Mordecai Richler as "imaginative and informed by intelligence." The title story in *Sunday Drive to Gun Club Road* was shortlisted for the Carter V. Cooper Award and will appear in the *CVC9* anthology in 2021. Quednau lives on the Sunshine Coast, BC.